THE LADY'S CHRISTMAS KISS

CHRISTMAS KISSES (BOOK 1)

ROSE PEARSON

THE LADY'S CHRISTMAS KISS

Christmas Kisses

(Book 1)

By

Rose Pearson

© Copyright 2022 by Rose Pearson - All rights reserved.

In no way is it legal to reproduce, duplicate, or transmit any part of this document by either electronic means or in printed format. Recording of this publication is strictly prohibited and any storage of this document is not allowed unless with written permission from the publisher. All rights reserved.

Respective author owns all copyrights not held by the publisher.

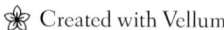 Created with Vellum

THE LADY'S CHRISTMAS KISS

PROLOGUE

"I have wonderful news!"

Rebecca looked up at her mother, but then immediately turned her head away. Lady Wilbram often came with news and, much of the time, it was nothing more than idle gossip; something that Rebecca herself did not enjoy listening to.

"Yes, Mama?" She did not so much as even look up from her embroidery, but rather continued to sew. The long, bleak winter stretched out before her, dreary and dismal – much like the state of her heart at present – and with very little to cheer her. Her father, the Earl of Wilbram, had made it clear that he was not to go to London for the little Season and thus, Rebecca was to be stuck at home, having only her mother for company. No doubt there would be a great deal more of this sort of occurrence, whereby her mother would burst into the room, expressing great delight at some news or other and, in doing so, remind Rebecca of just how far away she was from it all.

Although I am not certain that I wish to return to

London at present. There is the chance that he would be there and I do not think I could bear to see him.

"Rebecca. You are not as much as even listening to me!"

Out of the corner of her eye, Rebecca caught how her mother threw up her hands, but merely smiled quietly. "I am paying you a *great* deal of attention, Mother," she answered, silently thinking to herself that it was the only thing she *could* do, given just how determined her mother was. Having been quite contented with her own thoughts, it was a little frustrating to have been interrupted so.

"You shall soon drop your embroidery once you realize what it is I have to tell you." The promise in her mother's voice was one that finally caught Rebecca's interest, but telling herself not to be foolish, she threw only a quick smile in her mother's direction.

"Yes, I am sure I shall," she promised softly. "Please, tell me what it is. I am almost beside myself with anticipation." Her sarcasm obviously laid heavy on her 'mother's shoulders, for she immediately threw up her hands in clear disgust.

"Well, if you must behave so, then I shall not tell you the contents of this letter. You shall not know of it! And *I* shall be the one to go to the Duke's Christmas... affair."

Rebecca blinked, her gaze still fixed down upon her embroidery, but her hand stilling on the needle. Had she heard her mother correctly? Had she, in fact, said the words Duke and Christmas? Her stomach tightened perceptively, and she looked up, her irritation suddenly forgotten.

"*Now* I have your attention."

Her mother's eyebrows lifted and Rebecca set her embroidery down completely, her hands going to her lap. "Yes, Mama, now you have my attention," This was said rather quickly and with a slight flippancy, which Rebecca was certain her mother would hear in her voice, but she did not seem to respond. Seeing her mother's shoulders drop after a moment, her hands going to her sides again, Rebecca let out a slow breath. Evidently, she was forgiven already.

"Yes, I did say the Duke – the Duke of Meyrick, in fact – and I *did* say Christmas."

"What is it he has invited us to?"

"A Christmas house party. It is a little unusual, for it appears to be longer than many others would be. But then again, I suppose as the Duke of Meyrick, he is quite able to do as he pleases!"

"How wonderful!" In an instant, the grey winter seemed to fade from her eyes, no longer held out before her as the only path she had to take. Instead, she had an opportunity for happiness, enjoyment, laughter and smiles – as well as the fact that there would be very little chance of being in company with *him*. No doubt he was either back at his estate or would return to London for the little Season.

"We shall have to speak to your father, of course."

At this, Rebecca's heart plunged to the ground, splintering as it fell. Her father had only just declared that he would remain at his estate over the winter. Even if there *was* an invitation to a most prestigious house party, the chances of him agreeing to attend were very small indeed. Scowling up at her mother, she turned her head away. Why had she told her something such as this only for it to be snatched away again?

"Even if your father should not wish to attend, there is no reason you and I cannot both go," her mother continued immediately, turning Rebecca's scowl into a smile of delight. "He will understand – and given that his estate is not very far from our own, the journey will not be a difficult one. Besides which, it is an excellent occasion for you to make further acquaintances in preparation for the summer season... that is, unless you have any desire to find a gentleman suitor this Christmas."

Rebecca laughed, shaking her head at her mother's twinkling eyes and forcing herself not to think of *him*. Given that her mother and father knew nothing about the affair and, therefore, the abrupt ending to what had taken place, she did not think it wise to inform them of it. "Mama, I am very glad indeed we have been invited. I go with no expectation, just as you ought to do."

Lady Wilbram smiled warmly. "You are quite correct. Now we must make preparations to attend this house party. You will need to look through your gowns and decide which of them is the most suitable. We have time to purchase one or two new gowns also, for there is certain to be at least one Christmas ball! You must be prepared for every possible occasion." Making her way back towards the door with purposeful steps, as though she intended to begin such preparations immediately, Lady Wilbram threw a glance back at Rebecca. Understanding that she was meant to go after her mother, Rebecca set her embroidery down and followed immediately, her heart light and filled with hope.

"Prepared for every occasion, Mama?" she asked as her mother nodded firmly. "What exactly is it that I ought to expect from such a house party? I have only been to one before and it lasted only three days. There was very little that could be done by way of occasion."

"You will find the Duke's house parties are very different experiences," her mother told her, grasping her hand warmly as they walked through the door. "You must have every expectation and, at the same time, no expectation. That is why we must be prepared for every eventuality, making certain that you have an outfit suitable for whatever it is the Duke might decide to do. Christmas is such a wonderful season, is it not?"

Rebecca laughed softly at her mother's excited expression and the delight in her voice. "Made all the more wonderful by this house party," she agreed, wondering how she was going to contain her anticipation for the few weeks before the house party began. "I am looking forward to it. It seems as though winter will not be so mediocre after all."

CHAPTER ONE

After being introduced to everyone, Rebecca took her seat beside her very dear friend, Miss Augusta Moir, whom she was very glad to see. They had exchanged letters quite frequently, and when news of the house party reached Rebecca, one of the first things she did had been to write to Augusta. How glad she was to receive Augusta's letter back, and how delighted to know that she would also be present!

"And that is almost all of us!" Lady Meyrick put her hands out wide, welcoming them all. "There are only one or two other guests still to arrive. I do not know why they have been delayed, but that does not mean we cannot continue. We will soon begin our festivities and they will join us when they are able. Pray, enjoy your conversations for a few minutes longer and, thereafter, the first of our games will begin!"

Rebecca glanced around the room, looking at each and every face and recognizing only a few of them. She did not know exactly who else would arrive, but the company here seemed to be quite delightful. In addition to the fact that she had her dear friend Augusta present also, she was quite convinced it would be an excellent few weeks.

"I do wonder what such festivities will be," Speaking in a hushed whisper, Miss Moir leaned towards Rebecca. "I have heard the Duke is something of an extravagant fellow. Perhaps that will mean this holiday house party will be an exceptional one."

"Yes, but *all* Dukes are known to be extravagant fellows," Rebecca reminded her friend, chuckling. "I would expect nothing less. Although," she continued. "I do wonder where the Duke himself is."

"Did you not greet him when you arrived? He was waiting on the steps to make certain that we were greeted. I certainly was made to feel very welcome by his mother!"

"Yes, he did do so." Remembering the slightly pinched expression on the Duke's face when he had greeted both her and her mother, Rebecca allowed her own concern to remain. "He did not appear to be very glad to see us, however. I will say that for him."

Her friend nodded slowly, her gaze drifting around the room as murmurs of conversation continued between the other guests. "He did not smile once, and certainly I found him rather stiff. His mother, on the other hand, was quite the opposite."

"Mayhap he simply does not like the cold, and given the Season, it is rather cold."

Her friend nodded in agreement, although Rebecca did not miss the twinkle in her friend's eyes. "It is almost as though he does not realize it is wintertime," she remarked, making Rebecca laugh. Her laughter changed into a sigh. "Perhaps he is as I am, in waiting and hoping for the summer to return," Her mind grew suddenly heavy, and she looked away. "I confess I struggle with this long winter. My mood is much improved now that my father has permitted me to come to this house party, however."

Miss Moir laughed softly. "And I am also grateful for your presence here. I am, as you know, a little shy, and I confess that not knowing a great many people here as yet has allowed my anxiety to rise a little."

"You have no need to be at all anxious," Rebecca replied firmly. "You are more than handsome, come from an excellent family and you are well able to have many a conversation with both gentlemen and ladies." She lifted one eyebrow. "At times, I think you pretend this anxiety is a part of your character, for I do not think I would be aware of it otherwise."

"I swear to you, I do not pretend!" Miss Moir exclaimed, only to let out a chuckle and to shake her head, realizing that Rebecca was teasing her. "Do you hope to meet anyone of interest here? Or shall you only be interested in furthering your acquaintances? Christmas is a time where many a gentleman will seek to steal a kiss!"

Hesitating, Rebecca wondered how she was to answer. Her friend was entirely unaware of how her heart had been broken this last Season. Indeed, neither her mother nor her father was aware of it either, but she had borne this heavy weight for many months. The pain lingered still, and there was only one gentleman that she was to blame for it. Her mother and her friends might be hopeful that she would acquaint herself with a gentleman of note with the hope that perhaps the match would be made in the summer Season, but for the present, Rebecca was quite contented to have only acquaintances – and nothing more. Her heart was still too damaged. It certainly had not been healed enough for her to even *think* about becoming closely acquainted with another gentleman.

"Lady Rebecca?"

Rebecca blinked quickly, and then silently demanded that she smile in response. "Forgive me, I became a little lost in thought." Shrugging, she looked away. "I think I should be glad of new acquaintances for the present at least. I do not want nor require anything else."

"I quite understand," Miss Moir looked away, just as Rebecca turned her gaze back towards her friend. Rebecca chose to say nothing further, waiting until her friend looked back at her before she continued the conversation.

"What do you think shall be our first game?" With a quick breath, she returned their topic of conversation to the house party itself. She did not want to go into any particular details about what had happened the previous season, given that a good deal of it was still a secret.

Miss Moir clapped her hands lightly. "I do hope it will be something that will make us all laugh and smile so that there is no awkwardness between any of us any longer." Excitement shone in her eyes, and Rebecca could not help but smile.

"Perhaps there will be some Christmas games! Out of all the ones you can think of, which one would be your favorite?"

The two considered this for some minutes and, thereafter, fell into a deep discussion about whether the Twelfth Night cake or Snapdragon was the very best game. But eventually, their conversation was cut short by Lady Meyrick speaking again.

"I do not think we shall wait any longer. Instead, we shall proceed to the library – but not to dance or any such thing! No indeed, there shall be *many* a game at this house party! Yes, we are to be provided with a great deal of entertainment during your time here, but on occasion we shall be required to make our own entertainment... as we shall do this evening."

Chuckling good naturedly, Rebecca grinned as Miss Moir looped her arm through hers so they might walk together. It appeared this was to be the beginning of a most excellent holiday.

"Do you know who it is that is yet to arrive?" Rebecca asked quietly, as Lady Meyrick spoke quietly to her son, who had interrupted her for some reason.

"No, I do not know," Miss Moir shot her a glance. "But I, myself, would not *dare* to be tardy to something such as this, not when the Duke and his mother have shown such generosity!"

Rebecca shrugged. "Mayhap those still absent are well known to the Duke and had always stated they would be tardy?"

"Mayhap," Miss Moir looked around the room at each guest in turn as they waited to make their way to the library. "I admit I am eager to know who else is to arrive!"

"As am I." Rebecca grinned at her friend just as Lady Meyrick clapped her hands brightly, catching everyone's attention again. The bright smile on the lady's face reflected the joy and anticipation in Rebecca's heart as she waited to hear what it was they were to do.

"We shall begin by playing ourselves a few hands of cards. However, it shall be a little different, for there will be forfeits for those who lose, but gifts for the winner!"

This was met by murmurs of excitement as Rebecca's heart skipped a beat in a thrill of anticipation. She was already looking forward to the game, wondering whether she would have any chance of winning, and if she did, what the gift she would receive might be. A million ideas went through her mind as she battled to catch her breath. There was often a good deal less consideration to propriety and society's customs at such occasions, according to her mother. They were a good deal freer, no longer bound by a set of strict and rigid rules. This was a chance to laugh, to make merry and to enjoy every moment of being here. She was already looking forward to it.

"If you would like to make your way through to the library, the card tables have already been set out."

Unwilling to show any great eagerness for fear of being teased about it by either her mother or her friend, Rebecca stood quietly but did not move.

"Come!" Miss Moir immediately moved forward, tugging Rebecca along with her. "What do you suppose the forfeits might be?"

Rebecca laughed as they made to quit of the room. "I confess I can think of a great many things, but I cannot be certain whether I am correct!"

Miss Moir bit her lip. "I do hope I shall not fail. I would be most embarrassed should I make a fool of myself."

Rebecca pressed her friend's hand. "I do not think you need to have any fear in that regard, my dear friend. The forfeits will not be severe. They may make us a little embarrassed, but it is all in good humor. At least, that is what my mother has told me!"

At this, Miss Moir let out a long breath. "I understand. There will be nothing of any severity."

"Nothing." Rebecca smiled as she walked into the library. "Absolutely. In fact, I do believe there will be nothing in all the time we reside here that should bring you any shame, embarrassment, upset, or anger."

With a smile still upon her face, she walked directly into the room, only to come to a sudden halt. To her utter horror, she perceived a gentleman standing directly opposite her, a gentleman whom she recognized immediately but whom she had vowed never to see again. Her breath hitched as she looked directly at him.

Surely it could not be. Fate would not be so cruel to demand this of her, would not take such a happy occasion and quite ruin it by his presence, would it? And yet, it appeared she was to have such misfortune, for the one gentleman sitting there was the one who had broken her heart. The gentleman who had taken all from her, who had left her with nothing – and at the end, begged her to keep it from the ears and eyes of the *ton*. A gentleman who now went pale as he realized who she was, a shadow in his eyes as he looked at her.

And everything suddenly went very cold indeed.

CHAPTER TWO

And in that one single moment, everything seemed to still. Even the air in his lungs refused to move, making it impossible to either breathe in or out. How was it she was here? How could it be that Lady Rebecca was present at the Duke of Meyrick's house party? When the invitation had come, Myles had been more than relieved, quite certain that Lady Rebecca would be in London for the little Season. It was his way of avoiding town, of avoiding society, and making certain his mother did not demand to know why he was not gone to London. He had come so close to finding himself a worthy lady, a lady he had come to care for, only for it all to be taken away... by his own hands.

Slowly, the sounds in the room came back to him, as though he had gone a little deaf for a time. It was the shock, he realized, the shock that still lingered as he stared into her face. The smile that had been on her lips only a few moments ago was now shattered completely, the light in her hazel eyes fading. It was as though seeing him was the worst possible thing that could have occurred for Lady Rebecca – and Myles hated that.

"I am very glad that you could join us."

It took Myles a few seconds to realize that the Duke of Meyrick was speaking to him, and another moment thereafter to form an answer. Clearing his throat, he managed what he hoped was a smile, dragging his eyes away from Lady Rebecca. "I thank you for the invitation, Your Grace. It is much appreciated. I confess I was a little uncertain as to what my situation would be, come Christmastime. I am glad now that I have friends to share this time with instead of lingering at home."

"If you are attempting to express some discontent with the Christmas season, then you will find you are not alone in that, Lord Hastings." The Duke grinned and Myles pushed away his frown before it could form on his face. Clearly, there was something about this occasion that the Duke himself did not like, but given that they were not particularly well acquainted, it was not his place to ask about such a thing specifically. Instead, he chose to remain silent.

"Indeed, you will find my own mother, Lady Meyrick, a good deal more eager than I to enjoy such a season," the Duke continued, with a slightly wry smile. "Knowing that she would give me no rest until I agreed to do such a thing, I now find myself hosting a Christmas house party, the length of which I believe has never been surpassed in all of society. Indeed, we are to have guests until after Twelfth Night!" This was not said with any pride, however, but rather with a heavy sigh.

A flood of frustration ran through Myles. Had he known that the Duke had no real interest in hosting such an event, then he might well have changed his mind about attending. Had he done so, then he would have avoided Lady Rebecca altogether! It now appeared as though he would have been better off in London. Keeping such considerations to himself, he smiled as the Duke of Meyrick offered him a brandy, accepting immediately, and without even the smallest flicker of hesitation. It was not as though he could depart now. He could not come up with some excuse either, for he had already written to the Duke with his acceptance, telling him he had no other business, nor any matters to concern him for the next few months, and therefore would be very glad to accept. He now wished he had not been so forthright in his letters!

"You will know most, if not all, I am sure," the Duke continued, gesturing to the other guests around the room. "Now, ignore my solemnity and frustration. My mother has already berated me for my lack of outward enjoyment. She has been the one to organize almost everything, I confess – although I did not make any complaints about that, of course." The grin was back. "If she wishes for me to host a Christmas house party, then I am more than content for her to organize every detail! It should be a great deal of enjoyment, however, and with many young ladies to converse with." His eyebrows rose in question, but Myles only grunted, having very little desire to express his complete lack of interest in such a thing. The truth was that he was still very much affected by Lady Rebecca, despite the fact that he had ended their close relationship. The jolt of awareness that had come to him when she had set foot into the room lingered still, sending tingling to his fingertips and warmth to his core. The Duke took his leave and Myles was left to his own thoughts – and could not help but allow them to linger on Lady Rebecca. Even though he was quite certain she had no desire to see him, his memories returned of the many joyous moments they had shared - the laughter, the conversation, the smiles, the dancing, and the closeness. He had loved every moment, had longed to be near to her. His only thoughts had been of the future – and then everything has been taken from him.

"Good evening. Lord Hastings." The sound of his name being spoken in soft tones made him start. A foolish hope filled his heart as he looked upward, only to come crashing down as he saw it was not Lady Rebecca who had come to speak with him, but rather another young lady of whom he had no knowledge. The way she spoke his name made him realize she had every awareness as to who he was. Evidently, they had been introduced at some point during the summer Season, but he had made no effort to recall her. Why would he even think about someone else when he had Lady Rebecca by his side?

"Good evening." Giving her a wide smile, he rose, hoping desperately for some flash of recognition.

"I was wondering, Lord Hastings, whether you were to play cards this evening?" The smile on her lips remained, and Myles sighed inwardly. He would have to give the appearance of enjoyment if he was to remain here, even though his urge at present was simply to sit and brood over his failings.

"I suppose I shall." His answer seemed to lift her smile even more, and she clasped her hands tightly at her heart.

"How wonderful! We have some spaces at our table and I was hoping very much that you would be inclined to play."

Shifting from one foot to the other, Myles regarded her for a moment, but saw no way out of his present situation. "It seems as though you are to have your request granted." He gestured for her to lead the way before he made it obvious he had no idea as to who she was. The young lady walked across the room and Myles followed quickly, glancing around one of the tables, which had three vacant chairs.

"Ah, I see you have succeeded, Lady Gwendoline!"

Myles smiled with relief at Lady Patterson, glad now that he knew the young lady's name.

"I am very glad to do as Lady Gwendoline asks." He sat down and then glanced at the other two chairs, just as Lady Patterson spoke again. "We could ask Lady Rebecca and Miss Moir to join us also, Lady Gwendoline? There are two spaces remaining and I can see that they are standing together talking."

"Ah, but we should not wish to interrupt them from their conversation." The words flew from his mouth before he could prevent them, in a desperate and foolish attempt to save them both embarrassment. "I am certain that if they wished to play, they would have seated themselves at a table already."

Lady Patterson rolled her eyes and snorted with evident disparagement at his remark and heat billowed up in Myles' face. Why had he been foolish enough to speak so?

"And you, Lady Rebecca, Miss Moir? Might you both be willing to play cards with us?" Lady Patterson's voice flooded the room and the two young ladies immediately came near. "As you can see, we have two seats remaining - which must be for you both. Unless, that is, you have no wish to play – as Lord Hastings believes you to be."

Immediately, Lady Rebecca's eyes swung towards Myles, who could do nothing but shrug his shoulders, trying to find a reason why he had said such a thing and coming up with very little. "I – I thought you were in deep conversation with your friend," he said. "I did not mean to assume."

Lady Rebecca sat down in her chair, her chin lifting as

she looked back at him, clearly having no hesitation when it came to looking directly into his face. Her light brown hair was pulled back from her face, giving him a view of her high cheekbones and the delicate lift of her brow. She looked almost regal. "And yet assume you did, Lord Hastings." Her cool voice drove ice into his bones.

"I can only apologize." He could not tell if she accepted his apology. She simply looked up at him for a long moment, and Myles struggled not to look away. It was difficult to hold her steely gaze, but hold it, he did, wishing that somehow she could see the sorrow in his heart. When she smiled, it was not one of happiness or joy, but almost a smirk. Perhaps she was glad he had made himself out to be a fool.

It is just as I deserve.

The game of cards began, but all of Myles' thoughts were solely on Lady Rebecca. Even though he dared a glance at her many a time, not once did she look at him, not once did her eyes flick to his. Shame tore at his heart. How had he ever done such a thing to the young woman he had come to care for and who, despite that, he had cast aside? Would she ever speak to him? Would she even permit him to speak to *her*, to apologize for what he had done? His heart told him that no, she would not – and he could not blame her for that. He had not thought they would meet so soon, but given how their last meeting had ended, he should expect her to respond with both disdain and even outright anger at his presence.

The game continued on. Myles hardly knew when his turn had passed, and when it came about again, and Lady Patterson became more and more frustrated with him, irritated that he was not playing as he ought. Again, Myles could only murmur apologies, having no explanation for his lack of awareness. He knew full well that it came from the knowledge of Lady Rebecca's presence – but he could not simply say that. Instead, he muttered he was fatigued after his journey and that, at least, seemed to satisfy Lady Patterson a little. Rather frustrated with himself, he felt a great relief when the game came to an end.

I cannot go on like this. I cannot spend the next few weeks in confusion and tension and upset. I have to speak with her.

Lady Rebecca smiled, rose and linked arms with her friend – and Myles let his gaze follow her.

She may not wish to speak to me – but at the very least, I have to try.

With frustration and angst twining around within him, Myles too rose from his chair and made his way directly to Lady Rebecca. The only thing he wanted was for her to be aware of his regret and of his sorrow – and that he had not known she would be here. She had to know he had not come here deliberately, had not known that she had been invited as well. Had he known of it in advance, he certainly would not have come – not to spare himself, but to spare her. She deserved this time of enjoyment far more than he did.

His steps took him across the room to her, and he saw her glance at him. The words from his heart reached up to his lips, but Lady Rebecca spun as he approached her, her furious gaze fixing to his as her friend stood beside her, her own expression a little confused. Lady Rebecca's arms folded across her chest, her hazel eyes narrowed as though she demanded he spit out whatever it was he wanted to say without hesitation so he might leave again – and at that very instant, Myles's mind went blank.

Silence spread between them for a few moments, and

then Lady Rebecca sighed heavily and then turned her head away.

"Since you will say nothing, I shall speak for both of us." Lady Rebecca kept her voice low, although from the astonishment on Miss Moir's expression, it was clear she had very little understanding as to what was being spoken of, such as it was. "You and I may be acquainted, certainly, but we are nothing more than that. Not now. Anything that has passed between us is no longer and, therefore, I should be grateful if you would keep your distance from me."

There was nothing that Myles could say other than to agree. It was the very least that she deserved from him. After everything he had done, he did not blame her for her desire for him to remain far away. Finding nothing to say and fully aware he had remained entirely mute in her presence thus far, Myles merely dropped his head.

"I take it from your silence you agree to my request, and for that, I thank you."

"There is no need to thank me." The words were mumbled through thick lips, and Myles immediately turned away, making his way across the room and being fully aware that those were probably the last words he would speak to Lady Rebecca for some time. This was to be his punishment, then. This was to be the consequence he would face for breaking himself asunder from a woman he cared for and who, he believed, had come to care for him in return. The guilt of it all sat heavily on his heart, but he accepted it, nonetheless. If this was to be his punishment, then he would not so much as breathe a word of complaint. He would watch Lady Rebecca from a distance, and his mind would fill with memories of her, of the time they had shared and how much he loved it. No doubt he would watch her laugh and smile and dance with other gentlemen and his heart would be torn all the more. He accepted it with open arms, nonetheless. He deserved this, he noted quietly, going to pour a brandy as the laughter and camaraderie filled the room. He deserved this and more, and thus he would take every drop of his punishment; every single bit of it and be grateful for it all.

CHAPTER THREE

"It has been two days now and you have still not spoken of him."

Rebecca gave her friend a wry smile. "Perhaps that suggests, my dear Augusta, that I do not *wish* to speak of him."

Her friend sighed and shook her head. "That is most unfair. You cannot have such a conversation with Lord Hastings in front of me and then not tell me about *why* you have said such a thing. There must be a reason as to the fury I saw in your face."

Rebecca took in a breath. It had been a mistake to speak to Lord Hastings directly in front of her friend, but she had been given no other choice but to do so. He had obviously had the intention to speak to her, had mayhap wanted to try and explain himself, and she had absolutely no desire to hear what he had to say. Yes, she might be reminded about the good spirit of Christmas and the many things that came with it - good cheer, laughter, fun and enjoyment but that did not mean she was required, therefore, to forgive Lord

Hastings for what he had done. His injury to her was far too severe for that.

"I am concerned for you." From the slight wobble to Miss Moir's voice, Rebecca could tell she meant every word. She could not pretend his presence here did not affect her. In fact, it was a constant, dull ache, being continually reminded of what he had done to her. The pain she had only just begun to escape threw itself around her again, pulling tight around her shoulders and her chest. She could not be free of it so easily this time, for to be in the very company of the man who had broken her heart would not allow her to forget it.

"You will not be able to hide it from me. You may as well tell me all." Miss Moir lifted an eyebrow and Rebecca sighed again.

That much is true, I suppose.

"I have not had a desire to speak about this to anyone, you understand." Keeping her voice low, she gestured for Miss Moir to come a little closer. "I thought I would forget about this entirely, come the summer season. I never once expected to see Lord Hastings present here. It came as quite an astonishment."

"Then there was something between you." Miss Moir opened her eyes wide, searching Rebecca's face for conformation and, swallowing hard, Rebecca nodded.

"Yes, there was at one time."

"But nothing was ever said." Miss Moir's voice was soft, but her astonishment was apparent all the more. "You never once told me of this."

"I did not tell a soul." A little surprised at her friend's vehemence, Rebecca tried to shrug. "As I said, it was uncertain as to whether or not anything of significance would come from our friendship, but when Lord Hastings spoke of our future, I was quite certain he was to go to my father. I was so excited, quite sure I could now tell everyone that I cared for Lord Hastings."

Miss Moir blinked. "You did not even tell your mother?"

Rebecca lifted one shoulder, a slight embarrassment heating her cheeks. "For our connection to work, Lord Hastings begged me to keep silent of it for a time, and thus, I did. Our friendship changed to something more – and still, we spoke of it to no-one. I found my heart was significantly changed toward him. However, he, in turn, changed towards me."

Her heart cried out in pain, as though she were experiencing it all for the very first time, all over again. Her breath constricted, and she looked away. Perhaps this was why she had told no one of her situation; she had somehow known the pain would be too great.

"I do not understand." Miss Moir looked a great deal confused, rubbing at a line that had formed between her brows. "Why did Lord Hastings have no desire for you to speak to anyone?"

"He would not say specifically."

Immediately, Miss Moir rolled her eyes and Rebecca tried to laugh off the embarrassment that came with telling the truth. "Mayhap it was foolish of me to accept such a statement without qualification. But you do not understand." One hand reached out to grasp Miss Moir's hand. "Lord Hastings brought out such feelings in me as I have never experienced before. I trusted him. I thought his feelings were the same as mine and that any reason for asking me such a thing was genuine intent and concern."

Miss Moir nodded slowly, her eyes a little wide still. "So there was a friendship between you. A friendship that he swore would be something more and yet when it came to it, he asked you to keep your close acquaintance a secret, promising that there would be something more in time."

Rebecca swallowed hard, her throat burning. "Yes, that is as it was. As I said, I believed his feelings matched my own – foolishly, it seems,"

Miss Moir shook her head. "I do not think you are foolish. I understand your reasons for wishing to keep it so quiet. It must be painful to see him, especially after he has broken your heart."

Rebecca was about to state she had *not* had her heart broken by Lord Hastings, only for her to close her mouth tight again. She had already admitted everything to her friend, the only person she had ever spoken to about Lord Hastings - and there would be no reason to hide such a thing from her now.

"It does seem as though he is willing to do as you ask, however." Miss Moir smiled gently. "That is good at least."

Considering for a moment, Rebecca nodded. Her stomach tightened suddenly as she caught sight of the very gentleman they were speaking of now entering the room. Her breath hitched, and she turned her face away. Even just looking at him just reminded her of everything they had once shared and now no longer had.

He will not come near to me. There is nothing that I need to be afraid of.

All the same, she felt herself suddenly uncomfortable, a warm flush rising up her chest and going into her face. Wishing she had thought to bring a fan, even though it was wintertime, the roaring fire in the center of the drawing room sent out a great billow of heat.

"I think... I think I shall return to my room for a moment."

Immediately, Miss Moir looked at her, her eyes wide and one hand going to Rebecca's arm. "Are you unwell?"

Rebecca shook her head. "I am quite well. It is only that I wish to return my room to fetch my fan."

This remark brought a deep frown on her friend's face. "Could you not simply ask one of the maids to return it for you? That is what they are here for, after all."

Having no desire to explain herself further, Rebecca shook her head, said she was more than willing to do so herself, and quickly left, her irritation a little stoked. It was not that she did not appreciate the lady's company, but the questioning could be rather tiring at times. In fact, she was a little surprised Miss Moir had not asked her more about her acquaintance with Lord Hastings.

Stepping into her bedchamber and hoping Miss Moir would explain to her mother should any questions be asked as to where Rebecca had gone, she walked straight to the bed and sat down heavily.

Something crinkled underneath.

Blinking in surprise, Rebecca lifted herself from the bed, turning around to see. Much to her astonishment, there was a note pressed to her bedsheet. Reaching for it, she took it to herself with a suddenly trembling hand. Who had entered her room in order to set a note there? Why would someone do such a thing? Was there to be some remark over her behavior? And if that were the case, then why had they not simply spoken to her of it?

Picking up the note, she turned it over. A small frown caught at her forehead as she inspected it, but there was nothing of significance, nothing that would tell her as to who the author was. Glancing around the room as she feared someone else was present, she turned it over and unfolded it quickly. Her questions remained for only a second longer as her eyes went to the bottom of the page, reading the name there, and finding herself so overcome with shock that she could barely accept it.

It was from none other than Lord Hastings - the man who had promised to stay far from her. The man who, in his own way, was doing what he could to make certain he not only kept his word but expressed himself to her all the same.

Sitting down heavily, Rebecca read over the rest of the letter, starting from the beginning. It was not overly long but everything was communicated clearly and found her heart yearning and for what she had lost.

'My dear Rebecca, I never intended to make this house party a difficult one for you. I know how much you love the Christmas season and would not have attended the house party had I known you were to be present. Your request for me to stay far from you will be both acknowledged and accepted, but I pray you will forgive me for this one letter. I fear I could not communicate to you all that is within me otherwise. My mouth went dry when I came to speak with you and my desire to explain what I could to you simply faded away.

I would like to express to you the regret I feel at ending what had been become so precious to me. Yes, there was reason for it, but I must have hurt you terribly by doing so, particularly since it was without explanation. That was never my intention. Perhaps this house party has come for a reason. If there is a single modicum of affection in your heart for me still, as astonishing as that would be, then pray would you reconsider your request for me to stay away from your side? Even if it is only to talk for a few minutes, so that I can express to you some of the difficulties that caused the end of our acquaintance. I would be so very grateful to you for the opportunity. I cannot tell you all but I will tell you what I can. I swear it. It is a request I do not deserve – of that, I am well aware – but it is something that yet, I would ask of you. If you do not approach me, I shall say nothing more. This letter will be my only communication to you for these few weeks. I would beg for your forgiveness, but I know it is not something that can easily be given, not when I have behaved in such a fashion. Therefore, I will leave you with only my apologies, having no expectation for you to either accept or refuse them. Yours, etc.'

Her breath was spiraling in her chest, leaving her feeling a little faint. She gazed down at the letter, her vision a little blurred as she took in air into dry, heaving lungs. How could it be that Lord Hastings dare write such a letter to her? What did he imagine her reaction would be to it? Did he think she would be glad to hear from him? That she would be relieved? The urge to go towards the fire and to throw the letter into it was strong, but she battled the feeling furiously. Rising to her feet, however, she held the note in her hand and looked down upon it. What was she to do with it? Was she to go to him immediately, thrust the letter against his chest and tell him it was much too late?

No, she could not do that. Not only would it cause everyone to look at her, but then there would be questions as to *why* she had done such a thing. Those questions would then lead to difficulties, and difficulties would lead to the truth coming out, and that was the last thing she wanted.

Letting out a small sigh, Rebecca ran one hand over her forehead. What was she to do? If she made her way to the drawing room again, note in hand, then no doubt, someone would notice her return. Perhaps Lord Hastings himself would watch for her. Mayhap he would expect her to appear in the drawing room and would know by her expression that she had found his note.

Her heart ached terribly as she glanced down at it again. What did he expect her response to be? Did he want her to throw herself into his arms on the promise he would explain all to her, telling him she had forgiven him? To do so would be to forget everything she had endured, would be to blow away the pain and grief that had come these last few months. To be left reeling with confusion, only to pretend such a thing had never happened, was not something she could even consider. Lord Hastings surely could not expect such a thing from her.

If there is even but a modicum of affection in your heart, then....

Rebecca dropped her head and groaned softly. That one sentence had set a fire to her heart, with her very soul begging her to look inward, to discover whether there was some such thing lingering there – but the force of her anger and upset, her lingering confusion and pain refused to allow her to do so.

No, she would not do this again. She would not allow him back into her life, would not let him become close to her, not when he had broken things between them so unexpectedly and seemingly without a single care over how she herself felt. He had not seemed to consider the consequences that would follow from his doing such cruelty and, in the time between their last conversation and now, there had not been a single note from him. He had not penned even a word to ask how she fared, nor to beg for her forgiveness or offer his apology. It had taken him seeing her at this house party for him to respond so and *that* was where she found her difficulty. If Lord Hastings truly felt such things, then why had he not written to her before now? It had only been since he had laid eyes upon her here that he had felt the need to write.

Taking a breath, Rebecca lifted her chin, suddenly knowing precisely what she was to do. She would make herself quite plain to Lord Hastings without so much as saying a single word to him. Holding the note tightly and refusing to allow herself to read over the lines again, for fear that her heart would reject the idea she had formed in her mind, she walked decisively towards the door. This time, it was to be her to make certain there was an end to things between them. Lord Hastings would soon realize she wanted nothing further to do with him, no matter how much he desired otherwise.

CHAPTER FOUR

"Now we are to play Snapdragon!"

The murmur of excitement and anticipation that ran around the room did nothing to lift Myles' spirits. He had seen Lady Rebecca quit the room and had cursed himself for what he had done. He had thought she would read the note in the evening once she retired to bed. He had not expected her to return to her room after dinner – and surely it was not that she had taken her leave of company already? Myles considered for a moment that he could not know for certain whether or not she had gone to her bedchamber, only for his nerves to return when he considered what would happen if she had.

That note would be there, waiting for her on her bed.

Only a few minutes ago, on his way to the drawing room from the dining room, he had stepped to one side, found a maid, and made his request. Not satisfied with her promise to do so, he had stood outside Lady Rebecca's bedchamber to make certain that his note had been placed there, his hope lifting his heart gently. As the maid quit the room, closing the door behind her, he had caught sight of the note lying patiently on the bedspread and had allowed himself a smile. He had shared his heart in a way that he would never be able to do in conversation – but now he feared she would read it in haste, would not allow the words to penetrate her heart and mind. In leaving it at this time, he had hoped it might give her a night to consider all that he had said. But now it seemed as though there would only be a few minutes for her to think about what he had asked her. He could not predict how she would react, nor how she would respond, and yet a tiny flare of hope still lit itself in his heart.

"I must say you look rather fatigued, old boy."

Myles cleared his throat and managed a smile. "That is because I *am* fatigued," he admitted. "I did not sleep all that well last evening. That is nothing to do with the Duke's situation, however, for the beds in this house are very comfortable indeed, are they not?" The reason he had not slept well was that he could not stop thinking of Lady Rebecca – although he would not admit that aloud. It had been in the depths of the night when he had decided he could not simply stay silent, staying far from her as his heart ached with both longing and regret. Thus he had decided to write to tell her of what lingered in his heart, so that she might know of his desire to share everything, to hope beyond hope she might feel something for him still. He was still trying to find out whether such an idea had been a foolish one.

"Yes, the rooms are very comfortable, but I would expect nothing less from someone such as the Duke." Lord Stone gave him a broad smile as Myles forced himself to pay attention to the conversation, rather than allow himself to worry about whether Lady Rebecca had found the note. He and Lord Stone had been acquainted for many years, and Myles had been glad to see him present. His friend knew nothing about Lady Rebecca, however, and it was that burden which continued to sit heavily on Myles's shoulders.

"What do you think of the house party thus far?" Lord Stone looked around the room, one hand spread out to every guest as though he were asking Myles to look at each one in turn. "I think there are a good many fine young ladies present, I must say."

Myles rolled his eyes, knowing Lord Stone's proclivities. "You cannot be thinking about anything such as that here," he stated as Lord Stone looked back at him with a grin. "It is only a Christmas house party. Leave such eagerness until the summer Season. As you yourself have said, these are all *fine* young ladies – too fine to be tempted by someone such as you." This last sentence was spoken with a twist of his lips, and Lord Stone chuckled as Myles grinned. Lord Stone was a gentleman inclined towards seeking what he wanted, and most of the time it was towards *warm* company. Whilst Myles did not think that it was the very best of behaviors, he could understand it so long as his friend stayed far from the debutantes and unmarried young ladies. As far as Myles was concerned, to ruin their reputations or even to *risk* such a thing was a step too far for any gentleman.

Lord Stone sighed heavily, although the glint in his eye remained as he poured a brandy for them both. "Very well, I shall heed you," he replied with a roll of his eyes. "And what about you? I thought you were considering matrimony last Season. Has something changed? I did often see you with one particular young lady, but that did not seem to come to anything."

A lump formed in Myles's throat. "No, it did not." He tried to speak lightly, but the frown that pulled at Lord Stone's brows told him he had not succeeded. "That was not her doing, however, but mine. I decided to separate myself from *all* eligible young ladies."

"And was that for any particular reason?"

Myles immediately shrugged, having no intention of expressing himself to anyone. The truth remained secret and would continue to do so, unless Lady Rebecca begged him to tell her. As far as he was concerned, it was better that way. He did not want to bring shame to anyone, even though he felt lingering pain over how unfairly he had been treated.

"I considered perhaps I was not ready for matrimony," he suggested. "I thought I might give it one more year." Wincing inwardly at the lie that came easily to his lips, he looked away as Lord Stone laughed aloud, making every other guest glance over at them. The sound rattled around the room – and it was then Myles saw Lady Rebecca enter the room.

His heart seemed to tumble over and over in his chest as she looked directly at him. Her eyes caught his, melding there for a moment, and Myles suddenly could not breathe. His hand held the brandy glass a little more tightly, his other hand curling into a fist as he stared back at her, wondering at her reaction. There could be no doubt that she had read his note. He did not think she would even have glanced at him had she not seen it. Just how, then, would she respond?

Lady Rebecca lifted her chin. Then she turned her head away and walked smartly across the room. The drawing room was large, with red wallpaper across every wall with the flames from the blazing fire in the grate seeming to heighten the color all the more... and it was towards this fire that Lady Rebecca walked.

Myles' heart immediately dropped back into place, his

shoulders slumping as he saw her scrunch something up in her hand, only to throw it quickly into the flames. She turned around sharply, obviously eager to hide her action from those around her, but again, her eyes went directly to his.

Swallowing hard, Myles looked back at her. Her eyes were fire, in competition with the flames beside her. It was clear she did not want to accept what he had offered her in his note. This was meant to be the end of things. This *had* to be the very end of all they had once shared. There would be no truth spoken, no explanation given. Even if there had been no resolve between them, he had hoped that there could be, at the very least, the smallest of conversations. But she had not offered that to him, and whilst he could understand it, his heart ached, nonetheless.

It is at an end then.

It seemed as though he was not even to be acquainted with Lady Rebecca any longer. They were to be as far apart as they could possibly be. A brief smile, a greeting, but nothing more. There could be no reconciliation. He could never have back what he had once gained, for *he* had lost it, and now, it seemed, he had lost it forever.

"And here we are!" The excitement of Lady Meyrick's voice filled the room, pushing hard against Myles's despondency. He did not want to play Snapdragon, did not want to go and join everyone else, but given the circumstances, he could do nothing other than what was expected. Lady Rebecca walked directly towards the table and Myles found himself going with her. He did not mean to. He certainly had no intention of doing so, but somehow, he found himself standing beside her, their shoulders jostling slightly.

"You can see that we have two tables." This time it was the Duke who spoke, rather than his mother. "Since we are so many, we thought it best to have the group arranged in two places. I shall do the honors at this table and Lord Stone, mayhap you would light the brandy at your table."

Lord Stone nodded as many shrieks of excitement and giggles ran around the room, but all Myles was aware of was just how close he was standing to Lady Rebecca.

He felt the warmth from her body down his arm. Their fingers brushed and Myles closed his eyes, sucking in air to starving lungs. So near to him, a reminder of the closeness they had shared only a few months ago and yet, now they were as far from each other as they had ever been. She did not want to know him. She did not want to be near him.... and yet that was all he desired, even though he had just seen her fling his note into the fire to be burned up into nothing but ash and flame.

"You do not wish to go to the other table, do you, Lord Hastings?"

The soft voice of Lady Rebecca met his ears, and Myles turned his head to look towards her. Her eyes met his steadily, but her face was rather puce, with no color in her cheeks. Myles, however, shook his head and then turned his gaze back towards the bowl.

"And here are the raisins!" Lady Meyrick stepped forward and with evident glee that spread a grin across her slightly wrinkled face, poured at least a dozen raisins into a broad, shallow bowl that sat in the middle of the table. Thereafter, she made her way to the other table and did the same.

Myles watched with a sense of heaviness in his heart. This was the antithesis of everything that Christmas usually offered him: joy, happiness, excitement, fun and laughter. It had all been taken from him, leaving him with nothing other than a shadow. To stand next to the women he had come to care for, knowing they could never be as they had once been was a heaviness in itself. He was heartsick, and that was a sensation he did not think would leave him for some time.

"And now for the brandy." With a whoop of delight, the Duke stepped forward to pour brandy into the first bowl and then into the second. The raisins bobbed about the brandy, looking for all the world as though they were some sort of tiny creatures swimming around in the amber liquid. He dared a glance towards Lady Rebecca but out of the corner of his eye, noticed she was not smiling either. There was a little more color in her cheeks, however, and he was glad of that. He did not want to make her time here more difficult, did not want to cause her pain. Not when he had already done so much.

"I am sorry."

The word slipped from his mouth before he could even think of what it was he was trying to say, and Lady Rebecca turned at once to face him. Her arms went to fold lightly across her chest, one eyebrow arching upwards.

"You are sorry," she repeated as Myles nodded, relieved she was keeping her voice low. "I want to ask what it is you are sorry for?"

"I am sorry for writing that note to you if it has brought you so much displeasure. I did not mean to cause you pain. I did not mean to add to your frustrations by my overzealous determinations. I wanted very much to express myself to you but given that you had asked me to stay far from you, that was the only way I could think to do it." His voice was no more than a murmur on the last bit, and to his surprise, Lady Rebecca began to blink rapidly, as though she were pushing tears away.

"And I thought to myself that you might apologize to me in person from what you had done," she said softly, turning away from him again as the brandy was lit. "But no, it is an apology because of the note I received from you. That is all. The first time we spoke, Lord Hastings, you said very little to me. I know I was vehement in my desire for you to stay back from me, but you have never once sought me out to apologize for what you did. You have never written a note to me until this very day, this very weekend, where we are together. It did not seem to occur to you to do so before this moment and *that* is why I have thrown your note into the fire. That is why I will not give it any further consideration, because it is not worthy. *You* are not worthy."

The anger in her eyes set her cheeks alight, and Myles caught his breath as the conversation and laughter from the other guests ran around them. Lady Rebecca was so very beautiful, even in anger. He moved a little closer, even though they were standing as close as could be already. His hand found hers, and he held it for a moment, astonished when she swung her face towards him. She did not pull away, did not say a word, but instead, simply looked back into his face. As he held her gaze, the anger faded from her expression and a softness reappeared – a softness he had not seen since the day he had first laid eyes on her. Boldly, he allowed his thumb to run over and back across her hand, and Lady Rebecca still said nothing nor pulled her hand away. She did not decide to move to another table, or to place herself at a different part of the table so that she might stand further away from him. Instead, she simply remained where she was, and to Myles' mind, it was as though the rest of the guests were no longer present. Snapdragon was not about to be played at all. There was no laughter, conversation nor giggles all around them.

There was only Lady Rebecca.

"It is your turn, Lord Hastings."

The young lady next to him nudged him so fiercely that he gasped and clutched at his side, making Lady Rebecca catch his arm to steady him as guffaws filled the air. It was then he noticed that Lady Rebecca had pulled her hand away. She had turned now to face the brandy bowl, and he had no other choice but to do the same, given that this was what they were to be doing. As much as he wanted to continue looking into her eyes and to see that slow awareness growing in her expression, he could not.

"Are you ready?"

Leaning forward, he surveyed the burning bowl. Fire and flame leapt out towards him, heat billowing upwards towards his face. The raisins still bobbed around and with an effort, Myles centered his gaze on one in particular. Plunging his hand into the bowl, he made to reach for a raisin, his fingers clasping around something soft and squishy. He pulled it from the bowl and immediately popped it into his mouth so that it would no longer be on fire. His tongue seared, and he grasped his brandy glass, throwing the rest back, so some of the pain would be taken away.

Cheers went up from around the room and Myles smiled a little more, encouraged and a little happier now – not from the game, of course, but from the fact that Lady Rebecca had taken his hand and had not tugged it away.

"Lord Hastings has found success, Lady Rebecca," Lady Meyrick exclaimed. "Shall you find the same good fortune?"

His tongue, still burning a little from the extinguished raisin, he watched as Lady Rebecca dipped her hand towards the bowl. To his eyes, however, she made very little attempt to grasp the raisin, barely dipping her fingers near to the bowl of brandy. Murmurs of regret filled the air, but she merely smiled and shook her head.

The lady to his left began to converse with him, congratulating him on his success, but Myles made poor conversation, such was his consideration of Lady Rebecca. The game continued with at least seven raisins remaining, given his count, and Myles prayed that Lady Rebecca would find herself successful on her next turn. Looking back towards her, he made to smile, only to discover an empty space beside him. Turning right around, he searched for her, but as his gaze swiveled around the room, he could see no sign.

Lady Rebecca had gone.

CHAPTER FIVE

Why am I so foolish?

"You cannot be taking a walk this morning." Her mother hurried towards her, her hands wringing as though Rebecca was doing some dreadful thing by even *daring* to think about stepping out of doors. "It is much too cold."

"There is no snow, Mama. I shall be quite all right,"

"But there is a significant frost. If there is ice across the pond, then you might fall in and then what should become of you?"

"That shall not happen, given that I will not be walking on any ice, Mama," Rebecca lifted an eyebrow and grinned in her mother's direction. "I am, in fact, a well-educated young lady who is all too aware of the dangers of falling through the ice. You need have no concern. I will only be out for a short while."

Her mother tutted, turning her head away. "And you are to take your maid with you, of course?"

"Unless you wish to accompany me?" Rebecca laughed as her mother immediately shivered, clearly unwilling to step out into the cold. "I take it you would prefer to stay indoors this morning?"

"I certainly do." Her mother smiled briefly. "You shall not be gone for long, however, as you said. Are you walking alone? Or are you stepping out with one of your friends?"

"I am going to walk by myself for a short while. I have found these last few days very noisy indeed and would appreciate a little solitude."

Lady Wilbram's smile lingered this time. "I can understand that." Gesturing towards the door, her mother's eyes twinkled, assenting to Rebecca's decision. "I shall watch you from the window if I can."

Laughing, Rebecca kissed her mother's cheek and then made her way to the door. The guests had been given a choice of what they wished to do that morning. Many of the ladies were busy making decorations to adorn the house, whilst a good many of the gentleman were having some deep discussions about something that Rebecca had very little interest in, all to do with crops and estate management. No doubt some would be eager to join the ladies after a time – and for a moment, Rebecca wondered whether Lord Hastings would do so. After she had burned his note in his sight, then would he simply go on to consider someone else? Someone to step into the place she herself had been in not all that long ago?

A little surprised at the pain that shot through her heart at such a thought, Rebecca shook her head and lifted her chin, determined to leave Lord Hastings back at the manor house rather than carry him out of doors in her thoughts. Stepping outside, she took in a deep breath and allowed the first full breath of cold winter air to fill her lungs.

A genuine smile crossed her face as she wandered into the estate grounds, glad to now be outside rather than in the stuffy parlor or drawing room with the other guests. The grass crunched under her feet as she made her way towards a small stone path, uncertain as to where it led, but quite certain she could make her way back when the time came. The Duke had assured her that the grounds were quite safe, and with her maid in tow, Rebecca felt herself quite secure. She shivered a little as the cold air ran around her neck, whispering at all the little gaps in her clothing. Pulling her cloak a little tighter, she made her way further from the manor house, feeling her relief building with every step she took.

How good it was to be out of doors and how good it was to be away from the others, if only for a short while. She required her solitude, for it gave her time to think, time to consider – and with that came a sharp sense of regret over how quickly she had reacted to Lord Hastings's note.

She had not given herself time to fully consider what he had said, but instead had reacted in a furious manner. There had been a moment of pause, certainly, but she had pushed that away, only to discover that, when he took her hand only a short while later, that her moment of pause returned with a vengeance.

Perhaps she had been too hasty. Perhaps she had not let herself truly consider all that it was he offered her. It had been the opportunity to find out the truth – or some of it, at least, as well as perhaps why their connection had been required to be secret in the first place.

What was it that had changed between the summer and the winter, between the summer season and the little season? Why was he offering this to her now? Was it just because he had seen her again? It did not seem to make any sense to her, but now, of course, she could not simply go to him, could not return to his company and state that she had changed her mind, for she had made herself much too clear. And that meant, she supposed, that Lord Hastings could easily look for another young lady, should he desire it. He had offered her the chance to talk, to share and to understand – and she had rejected it outright.

Taking in a deep breath, she let it out softly and watched as it frosted the air. The only other sound was her maid's footsteps from a short distance behind and Rebecca smiled quietly at the solitude, wondering whether her mother truly was watching her from one of the manor house windows.

Mayhap Lord Hastings is watching me, too.

The thought made her frown. "It is not wise to think of Lord Hastings, not now." Muttering to herself, she passed one hand lightly over her eyes, hiding her vision for a moment. "The matter is at an end. How I responded to his note was perfectly acceptable. It is over. I must accept that."

What distracted her from her thoughts was the sight of something most unexpected. Not just one, but two gentlemen, both sitting on their mounts, with one facing towards the stables whilst the other faced the path leading back to the Manor house. They were speaking to each other and Rebecca moved slowly to one side, standing behind a large, thick bush so she would not be seen. It would not be proper to be in the company of two gentlemen, nor did she want them to think that she had been eavesdropping!

"Hoi!"

The sound had her looking back at them through the branches and, much to her surprise, one gentleman threw out his hands as though to knock the second back. The other gentleman recoiled swiftly, only he slipped sideways from his saddle and fell with a sickening thud to the ground.

Rebecca gasped, one hand going to her mouth. Her

limbs seemed frozen, and indeed, even with the maid taking a hold of her arm, Rebecca could still not move of her own accord. Her eyes were wide, fixed and staring as she looked towards the fellow, sure that the first man would help him. The gentleman on the horse seemed to turn his attention elsewhere for a moment before looking back to the injured man. Rebecca made to start forward, only for the maid to hold her back.

"Pray, my lady, do not. There could be danger here."

Letting out a slow breath, Rebecca watched in utter horror as the gentleman still astride his horse turned his mount in the direction of the injured fellow, unable to prevent the scream that lodged in her throat to escape as the man simply rode over him, so the horse's hooves kicked the man as he lay on the ground.

The maid tugged at her arm and Rebecca was about to yank her arm from her and tell her she had no need to do such a thing, only for her eyes to widen as the gentleman on the horse made for her direction. Terror clutched at her heart. Had he heard her scream? Had he realized she was hiding here? She stared with wide, horrified eyes through the branches of the shrub, her breath tight in her chest. He seemed to come towards her and then, at the last moment, changed course, going to his left. Rebecca closed her eyes and concentrated just on breathing before turning her head in the direction of the gentleman who had ridden away. She had not recognized him, but surely there could not be very many gentlemen who had gone riding this morning.

"I should take you back to the house, my lady."

Rebecca took in a breath but was surprised to find it was shaking. It seemed to shudder out of her, making her tremble all over as she looked at the gentleman on the ground. Her shivering was not from the cold but rather from the fear that ignited in her heart as she had watched the scene unfold. It had been all so unexpected and confusing, and yet she knew she could not leave the injured fellow to simply lie there. The cold could easily take him, and he could succumb quickly. Perhaps that was what the gentleman on the horse had wanted, but Rebecca was determined that his plan was to be foiled. She was not simply about to head back to the estate and leave the gentleman where he was.

"Go and fetch…"

Her mind scrambled to think of who she might call upon. She did not know very many of the gentleman present, and her own father was not here to be of aid to her. Her mother would most likely battle mild hysterics if she were told about what Rebecca had discovered and she certainly could not ask the Duke himself, for to pull the host away from such an event as this would be improper and could cause a great uproar – and she could not permit that, particularly if the gentleman who had done such a thing was one of the guests.

A name came to her lips, and she pushed it away. It came again, and she shook her head, silently telling herself that she would think of anyone, *anyone* – apart from him. But the more she struggled, the more it came to her that he was the only one she could ask.

"Go and fetch Lord Hastings. And pray, be discreet about it. Certainly do not tell my mother." Shooing the maid away, she hurried over towards the fallen gentlemen. His horse was still going back and forward, puffing and blowing in some distress. Fearful he would do more harm than good, Rebecca grasped the reins, unafraid of the horse. It was not the creature's fault that he was so afraid. Perhaps the injury to the gentleman had also injured the horse in the way he had fallen.

Her heart beating furiously, she led the horse away and looped the reins once, then twice, over a tree branch before hurrying back to the gentleman. The maid, much to her relief, had done as she had been instructed, and thus, it was now only Rebecca and the gentleman whose face she did not recognize. He was not present at the house party and she did not think they had ever been introduced.

Her eyes rounded at the sight of the red stains in the frosty ground. Pulling off her cloak, she covered the gentleman with it quickly and, after a moment, looked around in desperation for what she might press to his head. She did not want to rip her gown for fear that her mother would exclaim in dismay at the sight of it and ask her what it was she had been doing. That was not something Rebecca wanted to endure, and thus she looked around desperately for something else. The gentleman's face was very pale indeed, and the fact that he was not moving spoke of unconsciousness, although she was glad his chest rose and fell steadily at least.

In desperation, she pulled her shawl from her shoulders and, winding it up into a ball, settled it under a gentleman's head. He did not move, nor wince. It seemed that this faint was very severe indeed.

"Whatever was that you were doing?" Murmuring to him, Rebecca carefully brushed back the dark hair from his forehead and pressed her lips together, entirely uncertain what else she was meant to do. Looking back towards the manor house, her heart lurched with relief at the sight of Lord Hastings storming towards her. The maid trailed alongside him, but the man's eyes were fixed only to her. Rebecca rose to her feet, reaching out one hand to Lord

Hastings as he approached, suddenly desperate for just the smallest touch to bring her relief.

"Lady Rebecca."

His fingers brushed hers, but she clung to them, a little surprised at her fervency. "Thank you for coming. I did not know who else to ask."

Lord Hastings nodded, his gaze going to the man on the ground.

"But of course. I was glad to come. Whatever happened to him? Who is he?"

Rebecca took in a breath, suddenly unable to describe what she had seen and afraid now that the gentleman who had done such a dreadful thing was, in fact, one of the Duke's guests.

"Lady Rebecca?"

Bending down, Lord Hastings looked up at her, his hand still grasping hers.

"I do not know who he is. He – he bled when he fell and hit his head at the ground." Wringing her hands, she looked down at him. "I do not know what else I am to do. I have covered him with a cloak and put my shawl under his head, but –"

"Which means you must be very cold indeed!" Quickly pulling off his own coat, he rose and flung it around her shoulders, his eyes holding hers for a moment. "I am sorry I did not do this immediately. I should have seen that you were cold."

A wry smile pulled at her mouth as she snuggled into the warmth of his coat. "It is quite alright. I was a little overwhelmed also by what took place – the darkness of it..." A shudder took over her frame and she closed her eyes.

His hand pressed hers lightly and when she opened her eyes, his brown eyes were searching hers, his thick, dark hair dancing across his forehead. "Why do you not go back into the house? I will look after this man."

Rebecca shivered violently and was about to protest only for her maid to murmur a vague encouragement. Her gaze went to the man again, wondering exactly who he was and what had happened. If he awoke, then would she not be able to ask him? "What is it you will do for him? He needs a surgeon."

"Have no doubt, my lady, I will make sure that he is well taken care of."

Rebecca found herself being led into the manor house by her maid, no other words spoken between herself and Lord Hastings. She did not realize how cold she was until she stepped inside. Shivering again, more violently this time, she closed her eyes and took in a breath, thinking about all she had witnessed. Who was it that had injured that man – and why had he done so deliberately?

Her forehead furrowed in a frown as she thought of how quickly Lord Hastings had attended her. He had not even had a second thought about coming to her aid. She had asked him, and thus he had appeared. It was as though he had forgotten everything that had happened previously, had set aside the fact that she had taken his note and crushed it into pieces before burning it in the fire. A sense of shame began to lick up the side of her heart as she made her way to her bedchamber. She had thrown that note in the fire, knowing full well he was looking at her, aware he would see her action and understand what it meant. And yet, when she had thought of only him as the only one she could call upon, he had not let her down and had come to her aid immediately, without asking what she wanted of him. That spoke of his character, a character she had once admired, only for her to believe he was not as he had appeared. After all, why would a gentleman with such character break their close connection asunder – and without explanation? To her mind, that was not the appearance of a gentleman, and she had held that belief for many a day... except that his actions this afternoon had shown her she might well be wrong about what she had believed of him.

It was all so very troubling.

Shaking her head, she pushed open the door to her bedchamber, only to start violently as her mother stepped forward, her hands flapping.

"I should not have allowed you to walk out on the grounds. You look chilled and you have been out for far too long."

Rebecca blinked in surprise. She had not expected her mother to be standing in the midst of her bedchamber, waiting for her to return. With a glance at the clock, Rebecca realized her mother was quite right to be so concerned. It was almost luncheon! Had time gone so quickly?

"The Duke will be expecting us all soon enough, and your lips are blue and your skin so very pale that he or his mother will think you are ill!" Coming across the room, she grasped Rebecca's hands and then tugged her towards the fire. "Even your hands are chilled. Good gracious, I simply cannot trust you!"

A little defensive, Rebecca scowled. "You can trust me, Mama. I only took a short walk out onto the grounds. It is not as though anyone could have accosted me, for the Duke himself has reassured us all that these grounds are quite safe. Besides which, I had my maid with me, did I not? If anything untoward had occurred, then I would have simply sent her back to the house for someone else." Rebecca noted to herself that she had done that very thing and the smile she gave her mother was a rather rueful one, even if her mother did not recognize it to be so.

"All the same, I think you a little foolish to have stayed out of doors for so long, especially when you know we must look our best, as we always do, for the Duke's luncheon." Sitting opposite Rebecca, her mother tilted her head, her eyes becoming a little softer with concern. "Are you truly quite all right? I should like it if you did not look so pale."

"I shall recover soon enough. I am certain the weather becomes cooler with every day that passes, but after Christmas, perhaps it shall be a little warmer." This was said in a light tone and much to Rebecca's relief, her mother smiled.

"Very well. Perhaps I should not have been so stern, but one day, perhaps you will understand the concern of a mother when she sees her daughter walking into the house with a face as pale as the moon and lips that are turning purple," She lifted her eyebrow and Rebecca could not help but laugh.

"I understand, Mama."

"Very good." The lady smiled and then rose from her chair. "I must say, I did find it surprising that Lord Hastings quit the room so very quickly when you were out of doors," she murmured, clearly half speaking to herself. "I do not think I fully understood what it was he was doing, although he gave some hurried excuse. He did not return by the time I came to the bedchamber looking for you."

"What do you mean, Mama?"

Her mother glanced over at her as she idly made her way to the window, leaving Rebecca to continue warming herself by the fire. "Only that I have never seen a gentleman move so very quickly, for he practically *ran* from the room as though something – or someone – was threatening him, even though we were only playing a game of cards! I do hope all is well. I should not want anything to ruin this house party, for it has been so very enjoyable thus far."

Rebecca murmured her agreement, looking away from her mother and refusing to allow herself to say anything. She imagined Lord Hastings getting to his feet and hurrying from the room in such a haste that even her own mother had taken note of it. She wondered what it was he would have done with the unconscious fellow on the garden grounds, resisting the urge to go to the window to look out to see if she could spy him. It appeared her agreement with him to stay far from each other was going to have to end, for she simply *had* to know what had taken place, and no doubt Lord Hastings would want to hear exactly what she had seen. Her stomach rolled as she recalled the injured gentleman, remembering how the other gentleman had watched the first fall but thereafter, had sought to trample him with his horse. That had been a deliberate act, perhaps meant to not only injure but even to kill the gentleman! Why would a man do such a thing as that? And on the Duke's estate, no less? Taking a deep breath, she clasped her hands in her lap, trying not to let fear grasp a hold of her. Whatever it was she had witnessed, there was an explanation. Silently, she prayed that once the unconscious gentleman recovered enough, he would tell them the truth about it all, so that they might find the perpetrator and he would face justice. Then, perhaps, she could forget all about it and enjoy the Christmas season once more.

CHAPTER SIX

"Where am I?"

Turning quickly, Myles stepped back towards the bed where the unfortunate fellow lay. "You are in the house of the Duke of Meyrick," he said quickly. "You were injured quite severely."

The man's face was still very pale, but at least there was no further bleeding. Myles had quietly arranged for the man to be brought into the house and settled in one of the empty servant's bedchambers, meaning the gentleman would not be discovered by anyone. A fire had been lit, and the room warmed quickly, during which Myles had dispatched a servant to find and bring a doctor to the house. Having completed his examinations, the doctor had stated the injury was not as severe as it appeared, although time would be required for the man to rest and recover. Bruises from the horse's hooves would heal, although apparently, this fellow had been very fortunate indeed not to have sustained any further, more serious injuries. Myles had sent the doctor away with the promise that he would pay the bill for the gentleman, not wanting the Duke to be troubled in any way.

"Why am I here?" Trying to push himself up on both elbows, the man squeezed his eyes shut in a haze of pain before dropping himself back down.

"I would not think about moving yourself at present," Myles said quietly. "I think you may have fallen from your horse and hit your head on the ground. There has been an injury to it, although it is not overly severe. There was some bleeding, but the doctor did not think that you would require anything further, although you must take your time to recover and rest. You are in the Duke of Meyrick's home and your horse is currently in his stables."

The man blinked. "I see."

"Might I ask if you know the Duke?"

The man's eyes closed. "I was invited to his Christmas house party but was delayed at home by some business affairs. I thought to attend later, although I am a little tardy now."

"Well, you are present now, at least." Summoning the footman who stood by the door, Myles gestured for him to come forward. "I will have the footman tell the Duke you have arrived. What is your name?"

Swallowing hard, the man's eyes opened again, his jaw a little tight. "I should not like the Duke of Meyrick to know I am here, not when I am in such a state as this. Perhaps I might recover first before I speak to His Grace. I am certain with all he has to do, he would not appreciate the additional responsibility my presence here would bring."

Waving a hand, Myles shook his head. "You need to have no concern. The Duke is an excellent gentleman. He will not want you staying here, in a servant's quarters, and certainly will feel no additional responsibility, I am sure."

"No."

Myles blinked, a little confused. "No?"

"No, I do not want the Duke told of my presence. Not yet."

All the more uncertain, Myles ran one hand over his chin. Why would the gentleman not want his name to be mentioned to the Duke? Why would he not want the Duke to know he was here? It seemed most extraordinary.

I was a little overwhelmed by what took place – the darkness of it.

What Lady Rebecca said to him came to mind, and Myles frowned heavily. She had not been entirely clear, but now that he thought of it, was there some great evil that had caused this man to injure himself? Was that why he did not want the Duke to know of his presence?

"I am aware such a thing is a strange request," the gentleman murmured, his eyes slowly closing again. It seemed to Myles as though he fought desperately to keep them open, but had not the strength to do so. "I do have my reasons for asking for this. Besides which, I am more than certain that the Duke will not have noted my absence. He will be much too busy."

"Be that as it may, I still think it would be best for the Duke to know you are here."

The man's eyes fluttered, but he did not give another response. Instead, his request hung in the air between them both as he drifted into either sleep or unconsciousness again – Myles could not tell which.

Very confused indeed, Myles rubbed one hand over his forehead as he considered what he ought to do. This was the Duke's manor, and to Myles' mind, he ought to know of this gentleman's presence. But if the gentleman had begged him not to do such a thing, then did Myles have any right to supersede such a request?

I should speak to Lady Rebecca first.

Nodding to himself, Myles gestured to the footman. "For the moment, do not speak to the Duke of Meyrick of this fellow. I will do so myself when the time is right. I am certain you are aware just how busy he is with the house party and I should not like to trouble him further with this difficult matter."

The footman nodded and Myles, quite sure the servants would talk amongst themselves about the gentleman's strange presence in the house, shrugged inwardly and then stepped back. Looking down again at the unconscious man, he drew in a steady breath and then let it out again slowly. He could not understand what was going on or why this man should appear so very unwilling to allow the Duke of Meyrick to know what had happened and that he was here. If he had been invited, then what possible reason could there be for him *not* to tell the Duke that he had arrived?

Shaking his head, Myles made his way to the door. "Have someone look in on this man regularly and give him whatever he requires," he instructed the footman, quite well aware he had no right to demand the Duke's servants do anything. "I shall have my valet sit with him until he is conscious again, however."

So saying, Myles made his way from the bedchamber and walked to the servant's staircase, his hands clasped behind his back. This was a very strange predicament indeed. Being hailed by Lady Rebecca had been significant, but he had not hesitated for a moment but had rushed to where the maid told him she would be, and with the maid herself on his heels, he rushed towards the front of the house. He barely had time to notice how she had clasped his fingers, but now that he thought of it, the sensation was suddenly great. She had reached for him, and she had taken his hand. He had held it for just a moment. There had been desperation and fear lingering in her eyes, and all he had wanted to do was comfort her.

"Was she walking with that gentleman?" Murmuring that question aloud, Myles' heart suddenly burned. She had said she did not know who the man was, but perhaps that had not been the truth. Mayhap she had wanted to keep it from him so he would not be injured by the truth of it – but then again, she *had* called on him for help. She was not a cruel lady, she had not a single streak of it in her and he certainly would not believe she would do such a thing to him.

The bell rang for luncheon and Myles lifted his head. He was still wearing his coat, he realized. When Lady Rebecca's maid fetched him, she had obviously had the presence of mind to send another maid, who had been waiting for him by the front of the house, to his room to fetch his coat. He had been grateful for it, for it had meant he could first give it to Lady Rebecca and thereafter place it over the injured fellow. Now, however, he had no requirement for it. Catching sight of a passing footman, he quickly handed it to him with the instruction to have it returned to his bedchamber and then quickly made his way to the dining room.

His quick footsteps echoed along the hallway, but just as he reached the door to the dining room, he caught sight of Lady Rebecca. She was walking with her mother and her eyes immediately flared as they caught his. Myles cleared his throat, astonished at the nervousness that swept through him. Their close connection had never been made known to Lady Rebecca's mother or father, but that had been for his own reasons – reasons he was now ashamed of. The ending of their acquaintance had been for an entirely different reason altogether, however, but perhaps if he had been honest with her from the beginning, perhaps if he had been strong enough to speak openly to her father, then they might now be considering matrimony.

"Good afternoon," Given the turmoil within him, he found he could say nothing more, aware he could not say anything directly about what had occurred. His quick smile and the flash of his eyes in her direction seemed to be enough for her to acknowledge there was more they wanted to speak of, for she gave him a small smile and a tiny nod of her head, as though to say that yes, when they could, there would be a moment when they could speak privately. The smile made his heart sing, a fresh happiness filling him.

It was almost agony to be seated across from her at the dining table, as he continually found his gaze moving towards her – but yet, she was often looking at someone else. The flare of hope that had been in his heart slowly began to fade away. Yes, she had called upon him, and yes, he had been eager to help, but thereafter there was nothing for him to do other than to simply be of aid to her when she required it. He could not imagine that this was the beginning of something new, no matter how much he himself desired it.

Lunch continued at a slower pace - or perhaps, Myles realized, it might simply be his imagination, given that he was seated opposite to the object of his desire without any way of reaching her. Eventually, when it came to a close, he prayed silently they would be given opportunity to mingle without any specific arrangement being made – only for Lady Meyrick to rise, cheer and clap her hands excitedly.

"I have a most wonderful game," she exclaimed, her

voice high with obvious excitement. "We shall play Buffy Gruffy! The chairs have all been set out in the library and I thought we could commence at this very moment." Her eyes twinkled. "And indeed, there shall be forfeits and rewards. There will trinkets required – and plenty of soot in the fireplace!"

Myles could not help but wince at the thought of having soot smeared across his face. He had played many Christmas parlor games, and on more than one occasion, had suffered such a consequence. That being said, there were other forfeits which he thought much more pleasant. If he were given the opportunity, would he dare to steal a kiss from Lady Rebecca? Would she be angry with him if he did so?

"I do not know if we will have the chance to speak any time soon."

Myles turned his head just in time to see Lady Rebecca's eyes dart towards him, a small smile already fading as her eyes immediately pulled away from his. "How is the gentleman?"

"As well as can be expected." Catching her fingers, Myles caught a slight flush rising in her cheeks as they walked slowly towards the library – although she did not either slow or quicken her steps. Instinctively, Myles put out one hand again, but then pulled it back before it could touch her hand once more. He did not dare do such a thing purposefully, even though they were in a great group of people. Someone could easily catch such a gesture. In addition, he had very little idea whether Lady Rebecca wished for him to do such a thing.

"Then he will not die."

Myles shook his head. "Push that from your mind, Lady Rebecca. He is not in any serious danger. The doctor has visited and said he will need to rest for some days whilst he recovers, but that he is not in any substantive danger. I have not told the Duke, however, at his request."

"I am so very relieved," Lady Rebecca glanced up at him again. "I had thought that when one is trampled by a horse, one –"

The shock that ran over him caused him to stumble. Catching himself, he found himself staring at Lady Rebecca, heat pouring into his chest and rising to his neck as she stood stock still, staring at him.

"Trampled?" he repeated, only for the library door to be held open for them all, and the guests traipsed through.

"Yes." Lady Rebecca came close, dropping her head and keeping her voice low. "There were two gentlemen. One made a swift action, and that gentleman fell from his horse – but rather than this first man help the second, he tried to ride over the fallen gentleman and, thereafter, rode away!"

Myles sucked in air, a thousand questions in his mind – but there was no time for him to speak of things any longer for Lady Meyrick was urging them all forward – and thus he was forced to end the conversation before it had even truly began.

"You are all to sit," Lady Meyrick gestured for everyone to take a chair that was set out in a circle, and a little unwillingly, Myles did so. Lady Rebecca did not sit with him, however but was guided by her friend across the room to sit at the far end, sitting practically opposite him instead. She did not make a complaint but sat quietly and, to Myles's frustration, she did not look in his direction again. Rather, she kept her head a little lowered, her eyes on her hands as they twined together in her lap, with her shoulders a little rounded. After a few moments, Myles realized she was, in fact, rather weak with relief. *That* was why she appeared so.

It seemed she had been so worried about the gentleman, her body had lacked a little strength until this very moment.

I do wonder if she knows who he is.

His stomach twisted as he allowed that question to remain in his mind. He told himself Lady Rebecca could not possibly know who the gentleman was, given the shock, the fear that had been in her expression, as well as the fact that she had never mentioned the man's name. But there was still that concern lingering in his mind. What happens if she not only knew who he was, but wanted very much to keep their acquaintances secret? She might very well be aware of his title, but perhaps their connection had been kept private for some reason.

Myles shook his head, reaching up to rub at his eyes. It was foolishness that made him think of such things. He had believed in his heart that he and Lady Rebecca had felt the same affection for each other. He could not imagine she would have made a connection with another gentleman at the same time, and certainly not so soon after the summer season. Just what had happened with that gentleman?

"As I have said, we are to play Buffy Gruffy!" Exclaiming this with great relish, Lady Meyrick rubbed her hands together. "I shall choose one of you and you shall have to come and stand in the center of the circle. You will be blindfolded by my dear son, and thereafter, everyone on these seats shall rearrange themselves so that there will be no awareness as to who has sat where." She giggled as though she were a young girl on her first Christmas holiday adventure and Myles found his thoughts pulled away from more morose considerations as he fixed his mind on the game. "I shall lead the blindfolded person to the chair of someone. They will be permitted to ask some questions and the person in the chair must answer – although there is no reason why you cannot attempt to disguise your voice. This makes it a good deal more interesting!"

At this, a murmur of laughter ran around the group and Myles found himself smiling.

"If you guess correctly, then the person in the chair is the next one who shall be blindfolded without consequence – but if you guess incorrectly, then a forfeit must be paid!"

A great many exclamations rang out at this and many of the young ladies immediately flushed and pressed their hands to their cheeks. Having experienced many a Christmas occasion before, Myles knew all too well that such forfeits could be an incentive for quick kisses and gentle embraces. What about Lady Rebecca? Would she willingly accept a kiss?

"Might I suggest, Mama, that in order to speed up proceedings, we keep a tally of forfeits? They can be.... exchanged at the end of the evening." The Duke's eyes gleamed and Myles sucked in a breath with the promise of what he could gain. This, perhaps, was his opportunity to prove to Rebecca he felt just as much for her now as he had always done.

"An excellent suggestion," Lady Meyrick agreed. "Ladies, you must be prepared to give some trinkets for any forfeits required of you – although gentlemen can receive a face full of soot as their forfeit!"

Silently, Myles considered that, should any gentleman receive a trinket from Lady Rebecca in lieu of her forfeit, then he would do whatever was required to gain it from them so that he, in turn, might be the one to hand it back to Lady Rebecca.

The game began, but unfortunately, it was not for some time before Lady Rebecca was chosen. Myles had been waiting in frustrated impatience for at least half an hour, before finally, Lady Meyrick led Lord Kingsley towards Lady Rebecca. He could not help but smile as he saw her cheeks blush lately, and the sparkle come into her eyes as she answered the questions that Lord Kingsley put to her.

She kept her voice very quiet indeed – so close to a whisper that even Myles had to admit silently he would not have recognized it had he been the one blindfolded. It was to his relief then, that Lord Kingsley did very poorly indeed, and guessed not only one gentleman, but two other ladies. Neither of the ladies were sitting anywhere near to Lady Rebecca and, with a laugh, Lady Meyrick remove the blindfold and revealed Lady Rebecca to Lord Kingsley. He was very gracious indeed, shaking his head and laughing.

"What shall it be, Lady Rebecca?" Lady Meyrick asked, her eyes glittering. "The soot or a forfeit?"

Lady Rebecca tilted her head, then laughed as Lord Kingsley bent down, going onto one knee in silent begging that she would not pick the soot.

"A forfeit, then."

"I thank you, most gracious lady!" Lord Kingsley rose, clearly very relieved, and then handed his handkerchief to Lady Rebecca as his trinket. No doubt Lady Rebecca would come to claim her forfeit from him later in the evening, although what she might ask of Lord Kingsley was another consideration!

"Lady Rebecca, it is your turn." With a broad smile, Lady Meyrick beckoned Lady Rebecca to stand, and she turned the young woman around before placing the blindfold over her eyes. Myles found himself sitting forward in his chair, praying that whoever it was that Lady Meyrick chose, Lady Rebecca would get her answers quite wrong. That way he would be able to take the forfeit from them one way or the other, and thereby have Lady Rebecca's forfeit owed to himself. It was not the first time such a thing would be done, and he was certain it would not be the last!

Whether it was from the position he sat in or the look on his face, Myles did not know, but for whatever reason. Lady Meyrick's eyes fell on him and after a moment, she nodded his direction. Myles's heart tumbled in his chest as she led Lady Rebecca towards him. She was so close to him that Myles could reach out and touch her hand if he wished it, but instead, he gripped his hands together in his lap.

"You may ask the first of your questions, Lady Rebecca," Lady Meyrick stepped back and amidst the giggles from the other young ladies. Myles looked up into Lady Rebecca's face. She was smiling lightly, and even though he could not see her eyes, he imagined they were sparkling with mirth.

"Pray, tell me some of your favorite hobbies."

"Well, I very much enjoy embroidery." Lifting his voice high and wobbling it from low to high and high to low, Myles answered as best he could, giving her a ridiculous answer that made the gentleman fall about with mirth and the young ladies giggle. "And I very much enjoy practicing the pianoforte. My tutor says that I am doing very well, although I must practice my scales more often."

Lady Rebecca laughed, but her hands twined into each other. Myles wondered if she was a little nervous.

"And your second question, Lady Rebecca."

With Lady Meyrick's gentle encouragement, Lady Rebecca took a breath and then asked her second. Myles answered in a very similar voice and, after a moment or two, she asked her third. This time, Myles dropped his voice very low indeed, and the whole room erupted into fits of laughter. Lady Rebecca's cheeks went a furious red and Myles could not help but grin, quite certain she would be unable to tell who he was.

Lady Meyrick stepped forward again, her hand going to Lady Rebecca's elbow. "You have two guesses. What is your first?"

Myles held his breath. From the way she chewed the edge of her mouth, he guessed she had very little idea, and indeed her first guess was Lord Northwick. A murmur run around the room, and Myles closed his eyes. He was so close to getting a trinket from her, a trinket that could lead to them sharing a kiss. All it would take was one more incorrect guess.

"I am convinced it is a gentleman." She took a breath, pressed her lips together, then sighed. "Is it Lord Blackhall?"

Myles closed his eyes and sucked air into his tight, screaming lungs. Everyone around him was laughing and cheering and Lady Meyrick was taking the blindfold from Lady Rebecca's face, and all he could do was stare at her as she realized who it was she had been speaking with. The flush left her cheeks as she pulled a trinket from her wrist – a small silver bracelet – and handed it to him. Their fingers brushed, but hers were cold and Myles frowned suddenly. Inside, his heart was jumping and leaping for sheer joy, knowing he would be able now to do what he had long hoped for and yet, as he watched Lady Rebecca's eyes, his heart slowly resumed its steady beat. As she made the turn to sit back down, he caught her hand briefly, but she did not so much as turn her head. Myles dropped his head, no longer able to look at the retreating figure.

She was not as pleased as he. If she did not want this connection between them, then he would not ask her for it. His desire would have to be continually unmet. The hope that lifted his heart only a few moments ago was now dead and lying in the dust. His shoulders slumped, his head dropping forward. He would give her the silver bracelet back, certainly, but he would not ask her for anything more than a handshake. There would be no Christmas kiss. There would be no whispered moments – but it was all he deserved, for had he not shattered her heart in the first place? Quietly, he accepted his punishment and surrendered to the sorrow and the guilt that was his.

A kiss from Lady Rebecca would only ever be a dream.

CHAPTER SEVEN

"Is that truly your choice of gown?"

Rebecca rose as her mother came into her bedchamber. "Yes, Mama, and I think it looks very pleasing, do you not?" She turned around with her arms spread lightly from her sides so as to garner her mother's approval. Her gown was a shade of a velvet blue, for she was permitted to wear more than merely pastel shades during the little season. However, from her mother's expression, it was clear she did not think it suited her all that well.

Her mother wrinkled her nose. "It is not the one that I would have chosen, I suppose, but you seem to believe it suits you well enough."

"And it is much too late to change," Rebecca replied firmly, quite certain that whatever she had chosen this evening, her mother would have said she ought to wear something entirely different. Apparently, it was taking her mother a little time to become used to seeing Rebecca in brighter colors. "Shall we make our way down?"

Her mother smiled, and they fell into step together as they walked from the room.

"And did you have to give away many trinkets this afternoon?" Her mother shot Rebecca a smile as they made their way to the staircase. "I heard that Lady Amelia had to give away at least six kisses!"

Rebecca shook her head, although her laugh was a little brittle. "I certainly did not have to give away as much as six," she answered. "Only two trinkets, and if we had not played that game so many times, then I would not have only had the one trinket, I am sure! But I do think Lady Amelia encouraged Lady Meyrick to choose her on multiple occasions, for she seemed to go to her very often indeed."

Her mother laughed softly. "That is just as it should be with games such as this," she answered with a laugh, surprising Rebecca by her lack of concern. "There is always cheating at Christmas parties. I am certain that a good many gentlemen wished to steal a kiss from Lady Amelia, and thus she was forced to give her trinkets away. It may not have been Lady Amelia's doing, do you understand?"

Surprised at her mother's lack of evident concern over such a thing as this, given there was a great deal of impropriety over stealing kisses, Rebecca took a few moments to answer. She had given a trinket to Lord Burton and one to Lord Hastings. Neither gentleman had collected their forfeits as yet and therefore, she was feeling a little nervous over what would be requested.

"Lord Burton and Lord Hastings are both fine gentlemen," her mother remarked quietly. "No doubt they will collect their forfeit this evening, although, should you consider anyone, I would prefer it if you did not think of Lord Hastings."

Rebecca stopped walking immediately, the shock running through her, preventing her from taking another step. Lady Wilbram turned her head, a questioning look in her eyes, but Rebecca simply stared back at her as a dreadful fear suddenly grasped her heart. Surely it could not be that the reason for Lord Hastings ending their acquaintance had anything to do with her own family?

"Rebecca," her mother came slowly back towards her. "Is there something wrong?"

Reminding herself she could not allow her mother to know of her acquaintance with Lord Hastings, Rebecca looked away. "I am a little surprised to hear you say such a thing, that is all. I did not think there was anything wrong with Lord Hastings."

"No, indeed there is not." Her mother shrugged both shoulders. "I do not understand it, but I am aware your father has a slight dislike of the gentleman. I do not understand why, and I have never sought to ask him, but given that you are barely acquainted with the gentleman, it should not make a great deal of difference."

A cold hand wrapped icy fingers around Rebecca's heart. Could it be that Lord Hastings had ended their acquaintance because of her father? "That seems a very strange thing to say, Mama," she murmured as they made their way into the ballroom. "I have never heard anything untoward about Lord Hastings."

"No, nor indeed have I," came the reply, as though this was of no great severity. "Come now, my dear, let us enjoy the ball. There will be many gentlemen eager for your company tonight, I am sure, and the fact that the Duke has invited more guests from nearby will make this an excellent evening."

"I am sure."

In spite of the other guests present, Rebecca's eyes searched the ballroom desperately for any sign of Lord Hastings, but his face did not catch her eye. Instead, Miss

Moir came directly to her, a squeal emitting from her lips as she clasped Rebecca's arm.

"My dance card has four dances taken already, and I have only been here but a few minutes!" She laughed and shook her head. "I am sure yours will be so also, for the gentlemen are very eager to dance tonight."

Rebecca could take no pleasure in this, for her heart was much too heavy, much too torn as to what her mother had told her regarding Lord Hastings. The only thing she wanted to do that evening was to find and speak with him about everything that was presently in her mind – and what a lot there was in it!

Firstly, there was the matter of the gentleman on the horse they had to speak about. Thereafter, she wanted very much to beg him to forgive her for what she had done with his note. Once that had been discussed, she was eager to talk about what her mother just told her, wanting to know whether it was her father who had demanded he separate himself from her – for if such a thing were true, then had she not misjudged the gentleman most severely?

"You do not mind if we take a turn about the room together, do you?"

Turning to her mother, Rebecca managed a smile as her mother practically shooed her away. For whatever reason, it seemed as though the Christmas house party had loosened her mother's tight grip on propriety, for now she simply laughed and waved them both off, whereas, in the summer season, she would have been insisting on accompanying Rebecca, even if she had been with a friend.

"Of course, my dear. But do come to me at once if a new gentleman wishes to dance with you. We must make certain any gentleman you step out with is entirely honorable."

"Well, I do not think you need to worry about that,"

Lady Sutton chimed in, coming to stand beside Lady Wilbram. "The Duke's acquaintances will all be excellent gentleman. I am quite sure of it!" She smiled at her daughter, who looked up at Rebecca with a grin.

At this remark, both Lady Sutton and Lady Wilbram began to discuss one or two particular gentlemen, and Rebecca, also afraid she would hear Lord Hastings' name being mentioned, quickly turned away.

"My mother is acting most strangely, I admit," Miss Moir remarked, glancing back over her shoulder. "She seems quite at ease and shows a good deal less concern over my whereabouts than she ever did whilst I was in London!"

Rebecca smiled, keeping her eyes flickering across the room in search of Lord Hastings. She did not see him anywhere.

"My mother is the very same – although I do not want to complain about it!"

"And who exactly is it you are searching for?"

Glancing at her friend, Rebecca shook her head and sighed. "I cannot keep anything from you, can I?"

Miss Moir laughed. "No, you cannot,"

Another sigh ran from Rebecca's lips. "Something significant was said only a few moments ago," Rebecca told her. "There is too much to explain, too much to go into detail about, but I will state that my mother said something about Lord Hastings which has made me wonder whether my upset and frustration ought not to be centered on someone entirely different rather than on Lord Hastings himself."

"But he is the one who ended your close connection before it became something significant, did he not?" Miss Moir asked as Rebecca inclined her head. "Why, then, should you wish to place the blame on someone else's shoulders? It is not as though someone demanded that he do so, surely?"

Something kicked hard in Rebecca's stomach as Miss Moir spoke the words that tore at her heart and hand. "What if that is precisely as it was?" she murmured quietly. "Someone forced his hand."

"Then he would have told you, would he not?"

Her friend's eyes searched Rebecca's face, but the only answer Rebecca could give was to shake her head. After all, she did not want to tell her about her father's apparent dislike of Lord Hastings, for that might place her father in a bad light and if it was not proven to be true, then things would look very bad indeed.

"So you think he could not tell you for some important reason," Miss Moir remarked astutely. "I understand now why you would wish to speak with him so urgently."

"If only I could find him," Rebecca sighed as she searched the room once more, but still, she could not see him anywhere.

"Your trinket, Lady Rebecca."

Her breath hitched as Lord Burton stepped in front of her, holding out the small hair clasp he had requested she give him during the game. With a small smile, she took it back from him, wishing desperately that he had not chosen this moment to join her.

"And what shall you require, Lord Burton?" Miss Moir's eyes twinkled as Rebecca shot her a look, seeing her friend only lift an eyebrow. Forcing a pleasant smile on her face, she directed her attention back toward Lord Burton.

"Yes, Lord Burton, what is it you require of me?" It was quite common for most gentlemen to steal a kiss, but by the shrug of his shoulders, Lord Burton did not appear interested in that.

"I shall simply ask for my choice of dance – and if any gentleman has the dance that I required, then they will have to give it up."

Rebecca allowed herself a laugh, greatly relieved that he was not to ask her for anything of great consequence. "I am able to grant you this quite easily, my dear Lord Burton, for, alas, I have no dances taken as yet."

Lord Burton immediately clapped one hand to his chest in evidence of mock horror.

"But how can such a thing be? I am quite horrified on your behalf, Lady Rebecca."

"You need not be," Rebecca replied, finding herself smiling despite Lord. Burton's obvious upset. "I have only just stepped into the ballroom and was taken captive by Miss Moir almost immediately."

Her friend let out an exclamation of surprise at her teasing, and Rebecca laughed before handing her dance card to Lord Burton.

"Allow me to rectify such a thing, although I will say I am very glad to be the first gentleman to take your dance card. It means I will be able to keep them all for myself, should I wish it!"

Rebecca laughed again as Lord Burton grinned, appreciating his good humor. But when she reached to take her dance card back from him, to her utter astonishment, it was snatched from Lord Burton's fingers before she was able to grasp it.

"I am certain that I would *also* be able to add another name to your dance card."

Rebecca blinked in surprise, finding the words snatched from her mouth as she looked at the gentleman who was now studying her dance card, turning to glance at her for just a moment as he smiled.

"I – I do not think we have been introduced." She took him in, seeing the rather wiry figure, the dark hair and flickering grey eyes, as well as the broad grin that spread across his face.

"But we are at the Duke of Meyrick's ball, are we not?" he said with a shrug. "Not all propriety must be observed. I am certain that you will not be disappointed to dance with someone such as I, regardless of the fact that we have not yet been introduced." His gaze flashed towards Lord Burton. "I am quite certain Lord Burton will make the introductions, should you require it,"

Lord Burton folded his arms across his chest, evidently making it quite clear he had no desire to make *any* sort of introduction and that he found the gentleman in question very rude indeed.

This did not seem to turn the young man away, however, for he merely laughed and scribbled his name down for her waltz – much to Rebecca's horror, of course.

"I have only put my initials here so that my name might remain something of a mystery for a time," he said with a sly smile as he handed the dance card back to her. "I do enjoy being a mystery, I confess. Good evening, Lady Rebecca."

Swallowing hard, Rebecca looked after the young man, wondering how it was he had come about her name. Miss Moir gave something of an exclamation, her hands going to her hips.

"What an odious gentleman!"

"I quite agree," Sighing, Lord Burton shook his head. "No doubt he heard me speaking to you and thought to push himself forward." Lord Burton spread his hands wide as he shrugged his shoulders. "Forgive me, Lady Rebecca. I ought to have acted a little more swiftly,"

"Then you are acquainted with that fellow?" Turning

her head, Rebecca craned her neck to see if she could see the man again, but he was already gone into the crowd. "Pray, who is he?"

Lord Burton shook his head. "We may well have been acquainted, but I confess I do not recall his name, nor his title. You shall have to forgive me for that, Lady Rebecca. I truly apologize for my lack of recall."

"Good evening."

Rebecca started in surprise, having not expected to hear someone so close to her. "Lord Hastings."

His eyebrows lifted. "Did I startle you?"

She swallowed. "Oh, forgive me. You have found me in something of a quandary."

Although I am very glad to see you, she thought to herself, choosing not to say that last part aloud.

"A stranger just came to Lady Rebecca, snatched her dance card and stated that he would be dancing the waltz with her!" Lord Burton shook his head, and Rebecca caught the way Lord Hastings frowned.

"Is that true?"

Rebecca nodded as Lord Hastings' gaze fixed itself to hers. "Indeed it is. I stated we were not introduced, but he only laughed."

Lord Hastings blinked, then threw a glance over his shoulder as though he might spy the person responsible. "How very discourteous. I am quite astonished to hear it, and I do hope you are not overly upset, Lady Rebecca. You do not need to dance with him later, I am sure. No one would hold it against you nor think you improper for refusing a dance under these circumstances."

Rebecca shook her head. "Alas, unless I have my dance card filled, I do not think I will be able to escape him. He will come to demand I dance with him and since his name is on my card. I shall not be able to refuse, for my embarrassment will be much too great." Her stomach twisted at the thought of standing up with such a fellow, and she winced – but to her surprise, Lord Hastings suddenly grinned, a light coming into his brown eyes.

"Such a thing is easily resolved." Holding out one hand, he gave a small bow. "Might I have your dance card, Lady Rebecca?"

She gave it to him without hesitation, her eyes widening as she saw him scratch out the gentleman's initials and thereafter write his own name there instead. Miss Moir giggled, but Rebecca could only look into Lord Hastings' face, her hands clasped at her heart and seeing him smile as he handed it back to her. There was a softness there that spoke of kindness, eager to spare her any embarrassment. Again, the character she once believed him to have had flew back towards her and she found herself smiling. Was he truly a gentleman of honor? She did not think she could doubt it.

Immediately, everything she had wanted to talk to him about came back to her and she opened her mouth to do so – just as the quadrille was announced. Lord Burton immediately interrupted her intentions by offering her his arm, which, of course, she had no choice but to accept. Everything she had wanted to talk about was thrown from her mind before she even had the opportunity to say a single word to Lord Hastings... and once again, Rebecca was forced to wait.

∼

"Make haste, Lady Rebecca!"

Rebecca turned quickly, having been pulled this way

and that as she had stepped out for almost every dance. When she had returned to Miss Moir, there had been at least six gentlemen standing nearby, all of whom had been eager to dance with her, and her dance card had become filled very quickly. Determining that she would speak with Lord Hastings during the waltz, she went on to dance with the others, relieved to know she would not have to step out with that strange fellow after all.

Now, however, she turned her head as she was led towards the dance floor, scurrying in between various other couples who had stepped out, her heart beating furiously as Lord Hastings led her forward. When she looked up into his face, he was grinning at her, and she found herself laughing heartily.

"You were quite prepared for the waltz, Lord Hastings."

"Certainly I was, Lady Rebecca. I should not like to miss my dance with you, particularly now that I am stealing it from another gentleman."

She smiled up at him, only to be swept up into his arms as the music began. Instantly, every single thought was flung away from her mind as they danced around the ballroom. It was as though they were back in the summer season, as though she were in Almacks, back in London, and dancing with him as she had done so many times before. The same feelings rose in her, her breath catching slightly as she looked up into his eyes. He was no longer smiling, but there was no frown there either. Instead, he simply held her gaze, flickering specks of gold in his eyes. Was he, in fact, thinking much the same as she? Did he find himself transported back to everything they shared before? Was he thinking of the last time he had held her close?

As part of the dance, she was forced to step away for a moment, only to come back to him again, and in that moment, her feelings redoubled themselves. Her tongue darted out to lick the edge of her lips and, for whatever reason, Lord Hastings caught his breathe so sharply that she heard it. In surprise, she looked at him, but his jaw was working furiously as he turned his head away. It was as though he could no longer look into her eyes.

The dance came to a close and, with something akin to relief, she stepped back from him. His nearness had brought about so many great emotions and they were so heavy, she felt as though she were weighted as she walked. How was she meant to talk to him when her feelings were so clouded, when they pressed down on her tongue?

"Lady Rebecca." He offered her his arm, and she took it, immediately beginning to walk towards the edge of the room, back towards those who had not danced.

"Lady Rebecca," he said again, still frowning. "I... I did not expect..." Unable to finish his sentence, he let out a huff of breath and heat poured furiously into her cheeks.

Nor did I," she answered honestly, fully understanding what it was he could not put into words. "Thank you for being willing to dance with me in that gentleman's place. I am very grateful to have been spared from that and I am sorry if you were forced to be pulled from a dance with someone else because of your gesture towards me."

"That is not something you need to apologize for." A small smile tipped the edge of his lips. "I was glad to step in and no, I did not have any intentions of dancing with anyone else." Reaching across with his free hand, he let his fingers briefly press hers as it rested on his arm. "I was delighted to stand up with you again."

His voice was so low and so soft, Rebecca could not bring herself to look at him, such was the warmth that now spiraled up her chest and into her face.

Lord Hastings cleared his throat roughly, as though he had understood the strange tension that now simmered between them. "What was the name of that fellow who took your dance card? Have you had opportunity to find out?"

Rebecca shook her head. "No I have not." She let out a small, dry laugh. "Although I am certain we shall make his acquaintance again very soon, for I do not think he will be particularly pleased at having his dance taken from him!"

"I agree, but he shall have to accept that this was simply his own fault, for he cannot expect a young lady of quality to stand up with the gentleman she has never been introduced to, even if it *is* Christmas time!"

Making to say something, Rebecca's eyes alighted on a man who was slowly making his way towards them, taking small sauntering steps as a wicked grin cast itself across his face. Her eyebrows lifted. "It seemed as though my prediction is to come true, Lord Hastings, sooner rather than later." With her chin, she gestured to the approaching fellow. "*That* is the very rude gentleman who sought to dance with me, although I am relieved he does not appear to be angry!" She laughed softly. "Not being able to dance with me seems not to be too great a disappointment after all."

Lord Hastings chuckled. "I hardly think that is the case." His head turned towards the gentleman, and much to her astonishment, he stopped suddenly. Surprised, Rebecca stared up at him in confusion, seeing his brow furrow, his jaw tighten, and his eyes narrow.

"Lord Hastings?" Speaking quietly, she made to move forward, but Lord Hastings remained resolute. "Is there something wrong?"

The other gentleman ambled towards them still, but his eyes were not fixed to Rebecca, but rather on Lord Hastings instead. Slowly, Rebecca realized Lord Hastings knew this man, and she lapsed into silence as the second man came near.

"It seems you have stolen Lady Rebecca's dance from me." The gentleman tipped his head, but Lord Hastings did not smile. Rebecca found herself almost clinging to him, a little uncertain as to what he would say.

"I believe it was required, given your impropriety." Lord Hastings spoke quickly, his voice low. "Whatever are you doing here?"

The first gentleman chuckled. "I came to trespass on the Duke's hospitality for a short while. He has invited me to stay for a couple of days, which, of course, I accepted."

A sharp breath escaped from Lord Hastings' tight jaw, his expression still dark, and it was not until Rebecca pressed his arm tightly that Lord Hastings turned his head to speak to her.

"Forgive me Lady Rebecca." He flung out one hand. "This gentleman, this uncouth fellow who demanded that you dance with him without so much as a word of introduction, is not someone to whom you need to give even a moment."

The other gentleman made to say something, but Lord Hastings merely held up one hand, silencing him.

"All the same, I should like to know his name."

Lord Hastings closed his eyes briefly, his jaw still working furiously. "Very well." Opening his eyes, he looked down at her and Rebecca shivered. She had never seen his eyes so dark.

"Lady Rebecca, this is my brother."

CHAPTER EIGHT

Myles glared at his younger brother as he stood with a jaunty grin on his face. "Whatever are you doing here, Shelbourne?"

"I do not know what you mean." Shrugging, his brother spread his hands wide. "I have told you. I was offered a little hospitality by the Duke and I have accepted it. Besides, is this not the Season for brotherly affection? For goodwill to all?"

Myles scowled. "But that does not say why you are here in the first place." Watching as his brother's eyes swiveled to Lady Rebecca, Myles' gut twisted. He could not let him further his acquaintance with the lady.

"Pray forgive me, Lady Rebecca. Allow me to return you to your friend, Miss Moir. Thereafter, I shall speak to my brother."

"There is no need to do so," his brother protested, but Myles immediately shook his head.

"No. Lady Rebecca does not need to hear any further discussion. Not between us." Sending a sharp look at his brother, warning him not to run away during the time it took for Myles to return, he stepped away, with every belief his brother would do precisely that. It did not matter how much Myles had been forced to give up for his brother's behalf. Shelbourne simply did not want anything to do with him – not unless he wanted to call on him for help.

"You did not expect to see your brother here, I think."

"No, I did not." Clearing his throat, Myles turned his head, glancing over his shoulder, wanting to make certain his brother was still there. "I am sorry for his rudeness."

"And that is not something *you* need to apologize for." Lady Rebecca smiled at him, but it did not last for long. "You do not need to tell me everything, but I should still be glad to listen to you, should you wish to discuss anything. It is obvious there is some trouble between yourself and your brother."

A slightly broken laugh came from Myles' lips. He caught the shock in her eyes, and immediately, with embarrassment, apologized. "Forgive me, Lady Rebecca. His presence here has come as something of a shock."

Lady Rebecca smiled sympathetically, then touched his hand for a moment before they separated. Nothing more was said between them, but still, Myles could feel her comforting presence linger even as she moved away. Despite the fact his brother was waiting, he could not help but to look after her. Why had he ever allowed the influence to push him away from her? It had been one of the most unwise actions of his life, and he cursed himself for his foolishness. Turning on his heel, he strode swiftly back towards his brother, who, much to his relief, was waiting still. That broad grin was still on his face, but it was swiftly removed, given how Myles grabbed his arm and pulled him away into the shadows.

"You will tell me, and you will tell me *now,* what

exactly it is you are doing here." Aware he was speaking harshly, but having very little consideration for it, he glared ferociously at his brother, who yanked his arm away and shrugged.

"I do not see why I should have to answer all of your questions, brother. I have come to the Duke's Christmas house party, just as you have done. What is the difference between us?"

"Do not attempt to play games with me," Myles stated. "You know very well why I question your presence. You are not a fellow to be trusted. In fact, no gentleman who is even acquainted with you should give you a *modicum* of their trust. You have injured me one too many times, and despite that, and to my folly, I have given up a great deal to protect you, to restore you."

His brother had jabbed one finger into his chest. "And I do not believe for a moment you have done so solely for my benefit. You did so because you think only of our family name, rather than having any true consideration for me."

Myles did not respond to this, other than to roll his eyes. His brother had attempted to say such things to him on many occasions, knew the guilt that was attempting to be forced into his heart – and Myles had given into it one too many times. He was not about to be made a fool again.

"At least I think of our family line," he shot back. "You may pretend as much as you please, but I know that you do not give even the slightest thought to what our family name might appear to be to those around us, had it not been for my efforts. Have you truly no real awareness of that?"

At this, his brother merely scoffed and rolled his eyes, and it was all Myles could do to keep his temper in check. Shelbourne had never given any real consideration to anyone except himself. It should come as very little surprise to Myles that he continued in his selfishness, he supposed, but yet there was still a great irritation there. Another sigh from his brother made Myles all too aware that he was not about to get the truth from him, regardless of how much he wanted it.

"Very well. If you are to stay here at the Duke's Christmas house party, however long it may be that we must suffer with your presence, be all too aware, my dear brother, that I will watch you *most* carefully. Not a single action will pass me by and should you do anything to injure a single soul here, then you will have a great many consequences to face."

A frown caught his brother's face and, for a moment, Myles hoped he might discover the truth. But the next moment there was that familiar smirk, a broken laugh and Shelbourne stepped away. Before he knew what he was doing, Myles grasped his brother's arm. Words came to his lips, and he did not hold himself back, stating them quite clearly before he could think better of them.

"And you shall stay away from Lady Rebecca. Do you hear me, Shelbourne? You will stay *far* from her."

His brother held his gaze steadily. No response was given other than a gentle shrug and Myles worried his brother would now go directly to Lady Rebecca, rather than do as he asked, simply out of spite. Licking his lips, he watched as his brother took his leave, a heavy ache growing in his heart.

His brother would not know it, for Myles had never spoken that to him, but Shelbourne was the reason he had been forced to step away from Lady Rebecca. The truth was painful and heavy in Myles's heart, but he could not escape it. The awareness brought such anger and upset – so much so he wanted to throw back his head and roar with frustration. Instead, he was forced to do nothing, clasping his hands tight in an attempt to keep control of his temper. That was not something he could do or say in such a situation as this. Opening his eyes, he lifted his chin again. Somehow, he would find a way through the situation. It would be best if his brother could take his leave just as quickly as he had arrived, but for the meantime, there was nothing for Myles to do but face the situation, such as it was. No doubt he would have to tell Lady Rebecca exactly why he had behaved so... somehow.

"I have been foolish." Taking a deep breath. Myles turned his head so he might look directly at Lady Rebecca, but she was talking with another young woman and did not once look in his direction, but Myles was glad only to look at her. It felt to him as though they were slowly finding their way back to each other, but with his brother present, he dared not do much more. There was the great and tremendous fear that Shelbourne would behave with such impropriety that the entire family would be embarrassed, that his actions would embarrass the entirety of the group. What would happen then? Would Lady Rebecca turn from him completely, embarrassed that she was connected to someone whose brother was so entirely improper? He would not blame her, for he had long been mortified at his brother's behavior, but yet what could he do? He had tried everything already and Shelbourne had not changed.

With a deep breath, he eventually turned himself back towards the other guests, stepping out of the shadows. He did not want to draw undue attention towards the arrival of his brother. Perhaps all would be well and he would not have to concern himself unduly.

A wry smile crossed his lips as he considered the impossibility of such a thing occurring. Whenever his brother was present, trouble came with him.

It was only a matter of time.

˷

"Ah, your brother arrived, Lord Hastings! I confess I was a little surprised to see him as we are only a little acquainted and my estate is far from his – but of course, I was glad to express my willingness to have his company during this Christmas season. It would be most uncharitable of me if I would not do such a thing at such a time as this!" The Duke grinned as though he had said something quite ridiculous, but Myles could not so much as raise a smile. Of course, the Duke did not realize the problems Shelbourne could bring with him. Would it be wise for Myles, therefore, to advise the Duke to remove Shelbourne from his house as quickly as possible, or would that only lead to further questions?

"I did not inform him of your house party, Your Grace," Myles said quickly, suddenly afraid the Duke would think him responsible for his brother's arrival but the Duke only laughed again, throwing one hand in the air as though he were delighted to have been given the chance to spend time in the company of Shelbourne.

"You need to have no concern about his arrival, Lord Hastings. Despite the fact I had no intention of enjoying this Christmas house party, I find I am slowly becoming accustomed to having so many guests in my home. I would not say such a thing in my mother's presence but I will confess to you at least, that I am beginning to enjoy myself."

"You are very kind to permit my brother to stay." There was nothing else to be said as the thought of telling the Duke to be wary of Shelbourne immediately fled from

Myles' mind. He could not speak so, not now. Perhaps the opportunity would come later.

At that very moment, however, his brother strode into the room. It was only the gentlemen present at the moment, for the ladies were all taking tea together in the drawing room, and thus the gentlemen had been cloistered together in the library. The brash "Good afternoon!" that left his lips as he walked into the room made Myles wince. Another glance around at the other gentlemen told him they were all a little surprised at this newcomer, and indeed, the loud welcome he gave himself as soon as Shelbourne made his way around to each gentleman, introducing himself and interrupting many a conversation without so much as a consideration.

Myles knew it was time for him to depart the room. He could not be here and watch this. He could not feel the shame mounting in his chest over and over again. It was time for him to find another pursuit – and at that moment he considered the gentleman now resting in the servant's quarters, the gentleman who had been resting there for some days and still as yet, had refused to give Myles his name and had refused to allow the Duke to know of his presence. The fear that had been in the gentleman's eyes had been the only thing that had convinced Myles to permit him to continue on so. The butler appeared to agree with Myles' demand that this be kept from the Duke for the time being, given that it was so close to Christmas time, and also since he was already very busy with a good many guests. But that did not mean Myles had no responsibility. He felt it now, and he left the library quickly, closing the door behind him and striding far away from where his brother was, as though his very presence reached out after him, demanding that he come back.

Why did he have to come here?

Grimacing to himself, Myles rubbed one hand over his chin. His brother's presence was not a mistake. There would be some purpose behind it – the purpose that, as yet, Myles did not know of. Mayhap, in time, his brother would tell him, but that would only come when he was in difficulty *and* with his expectation being that Myles would aid him in it. That behavior repeated itself often enough, and Myles could feel the responsibility piling up on his heart already, knowing that when his brother required it of him, he would simply step forward and do as was asked so that he might preserve his family's honor.

It tormented him so.

Knocking quietly on the bedchamber door, Myles stepped inside just to see the gentleman in question sitting in a chair by the window. There was a fire in the grate, the room was warm, and Myles was greatly relieved to see how easily the fellow rose from his chair.

"You appear to be a good deal recovered."

The man smiled briefly. "I woke this morning with a feeling of strength returning to me. I think tomorrow I shall take my leave."

Myles quickly shook his head. "I would beg of you not to do so. The Duke of Meyrick would be very glad indeed to have you join our party, I am sure, especially since you were expected."

"And as I have said, I should not like the Duke to be troubled." The man turned away and but it was not before Myles had spotted a flash in his eyes, the same flash of worry that he had seen many times before when he had spoken to the man about staying at the Duke's house party. What was it he was so afraid of?

"It would not trouble the Duke, I assure you. He has

already added one guest to his house party within the last few days and spoke to me about how glad he was to do so."

The man turned back to face Myles. "And might I ask if the name of the man the Duke has added to his house party is Mr. Shelbourne?"

It was as though Myles had stepped outside into the freezing winter air, such was his shock. The fact he did not respond immediately seemed to confirm his answer, and immediately the fellow shook his head, turning away again.

"In that case then, you can be assured I will not come into the Duke's presence, nor join his house party," he replied firmly. "Forgive me, but I –"

"You know my brother." Myles took a step closer to the unknown gentleman, seeing the man's eyes flare. Obviously, he had not known that Shelbourne had a brother, otherwise, Myles considered, he would not have spoken so freely.

"You.... Your brother?" Immediately, the man closed his eyes and passed one hand over them. A heavy sigh emitted from his lips, and he sank down to the edge of the bed before dropping his head forward, his fingers going through his hair. "If you are coming to finish what your brother has started, then you may as well know I have no fight left within me. I shall give you what you want. Your brother has already proven he will do anything he can to get his hands on what he desires. He has made his intentions clear."

"No, no, you misunderstand entirely!" With dread filling him, Myles moved forward quickly, coming to stand only a few steps away from the man to make certain he did not appear in any way intimidating. "I know nothing about what my brother is doing. I will confess I am horrified to find him present here. I have spent my life, particularly these last few years, when I have taken on the title, bearing a great burden when it comes to my brother. I have had to chase after him, attempting to do right by those he has injured and attempting to prevent him from going down the various dark paths he has chosen – although I have been rather unsuccessful in the latter part. Despite my intentions to keep our family name as well thought of as possible, my brother seems determined to do otherwise. Whatever it is he has done to you, I beg of you to tell me it now. I cannot help you otherwise." A sudden thought wrapped itself around his mind and he caught his breath. "It was my brother who knocked you from the horse, was it not? It was my brother whom Lady Rebecca saw?"

The man lifted his head and looked straight into Myles' face. There was so much doubt and uncertainty that for some minutes, they simply stared at each other in complete silence. Myles could not berate the fellow for feeling such a way, for he had no doubt that were they to change places, he would be just as uncertain. Perhaps, he considered, the gentleman believed Myles was simply pretending, putting on an act so as to find a way in through his defenses. There was very little that Myles could say by way of dismissing such an idea, and thus, he simply waited in silence.

"You do have something of an honest face." The man shook his head and then dropped it forward again. "No doubt I shall be taken for a fool again, but-"

"You are no fool." Moving across the room to a small chair, Myles sat down. "What is it that my brother has asked of you?"

The man sighed. "He and I were in a game of cards. There was some coin involved, and I put down what I thought was a substantial amount. I lost the round, paid the debt, but your brother states I did not. He also tells me that because I have not paid him in some time, the amount I owe him has increased."

Myles closed his eyes. "The scoundrel."

When he opened his eyes, the man was looking at him with a slightly confused expression, and it took some moments before Myles realized why. The fellow was still expecting him to turn around and laugh at how foolish he had been to believe him. Grimacing, Myles rubbed the back of his neck, aware of the fact that this was not exactly unexpected. He knew full well his brother was such a fellow and now was all the more ashamed the man now resided in the Duke's house. Once more, he found himself in a quandary, uncertain what to do, but all too afraid of what his brother's actions would lead to.

"That is why you are afraid, is it not?" Myles asked quietly as the gentleman looked away. "My brother was the one who injured you. He knocked you from your horse. How did he know you were to be approaching?

"I had been invited to the Duke's house party, as you know." The man rubbed one hand over his face. "I do not know whether your brother was watching for me or if he was simply following my movements in order to gain this money from me. Regardless, I came upon him most unexpectedly, although he did not appear to be at all surprised when I met him."

Myles shook his head. "And that is why you do not want the Duke to know of your presence here, for if he were to hear you had been injured, he would bring you to the fore and tell all the guests about what had occurred."

"And until this moment, I was uncertain whether your brother was also present," the man finished. "I believe you, however. I believe you are as astonished by this as you appear. I must hope you are a gentleman of integrity, however."

Myles placed one hand upon his heart. "I assure you I

am and again, I would beg of you not to depart the Duke's house so swiftly. In fact, I do think we should tell him all. I have been looking for a way to explain to him the dangers of being in my brother's company and mayhap with your presence and your explanation of what has occurred, he will understand."

The man hesitated, looking away. "I... I am not certain. Your brother has threatened a good deal more. My mind is still on giving him what he asks for, regardless of the financial difficulty it will place me in. I may be a viscount, but I am not the wealthiest of gentlemen, but that does not seem to matter to Shelbourne. However, it is the only way to ensure not only my safety, but the safety of those I care for is guaranteed." Running one hand down his face, he kept his expression hidden, his eyes turned away. "I dread to think what he will do if he discovers that I have spoken to the Duke about him, should I dare to do it!"

"But he does not know you are here - my brother, that is," Myles said urgently. "It was not he who alerted the house to your presence. It was not he who made certain that you were brought into this house. You may not recall it, but there was a young woman watching you. She sent for me and I came as quickly as I could. Only she and I are aware of your presence, as well as the household servants, of course. The Duke does not know of your arrival as you have asked, but neither does my brother."

The Viscount considered this again for some moments and, despite the fact he had a great deal of urgency and a huge desire to say a good deal more, Myles forced himself to remain silent. He shifted his feet on the floor as he waited, his hands clasped tightly, his fingers twining together and *still* the man said nothing.

"This young woman who saw me." The Viscount turned his head and Myles nodded eagerly.

"Lady Rebecca."

"The Lady Rebecca," the man continued. "You say she witnessed what occurred. Was that purely by accident?"

"Entirely," Myles replied fervently. "When it comes to the lady, you need to have no concern. She was most astonished that she saw you fall, and thereafter, saw my brother attempting to ride over you. I believe it is God who preserved your life, for my brother's intentions were cruel and dark indeed."

The Viscount's eyebrows lifted, but he did not speak for some moments. Again, Myles lapsed into silence, the urgency to say something more growing ever stronger, but he clamped his mouth shut. To say anything at this juncture, he believed, would only do harm.

"I should like to speak to her before I make any decision." The man looked back into Myles' eyes and he nodded, even though he had no certainty how he was to get Lady Rebecca to this room. "I should like to know exactly what it was she saw, to make certain I have a witness to any charge I bring to your brother in front of the Duke. I wish to be clear in my own mind. Do you think that she will come? That she has a trustworthy character?"

Myles set out his hands on either side. "I can only ask. She is concerned about you and I know, would be very glad to speak to you. Whether she will agree to come, I cannot say for certain, but I would be hopeful." He rose from his chair, aware that whilst he had attempted to speak to Lady Rebecca these last few days, they had never been given the opportunity to have more than one private conversation and that and his intentions to speak to her about this mysterious Viscount had vanished when his feelings had risen to such heights that they had rendered him practically senseless. "Promise me you will remain here until I come back with either Lady Rebecca or her answer. I should not like to ask her such a thing, only to appear here again and find the room empty. I know you have a desire to flee, to give my brother what he has asked and be done with the matter, but I beg of you not to do so. Have a little courage, Lord...?" He lifted one eyebrow and the man opposite him sighed.

"Lord Richards."

Myles smiled. "Have a little courage, Lord Richards – and be assured that your presence here will remain a secret until such a time as you decide one way or the other."

Lord Richards took in a deep breath and then, after a moment, nodded. He appeared a little fatigued now, and Myles rose quickly.

"I shall leave you now. Pray get a little rest and I will send a footman to see if you require anything further."

The man nodded, but said nothing more, making to lie down upon the bed as Myles quit the room, quickly finding a footman and muttering something to him before returning to the library. His brother's overly bright tones no longer irritated him so much. In fact, he did not so much as a glance at him as he walked back in to join the other gentleman. His mind was fixed only on Lady Rebecca and how soon he could speak to her about what Lord Richards had asked. There would be so much more to say and explain, but this was the most pressing matter and might, in fact, lead to a way for his brother to change his ways for good – whether he wished to do so or not.

CHAPTER NINE

"I think this a very foolish game."

Miss Moir giggled as Rebecca tried to hide a smile.

"I do not think it is very ridiculous, although I cannot decide whether I wish to be found," Miss Moir whispered, one hand going over her mouth as Rebecca shushed her, despite the fact that she had just said how ridiculous this game of hide and go seek was. It was mostly the young women and the bachelor gentlemen who were playing, with the elder ladies and gentlemen waving hands and stating they were much too old for such joyous abandon. Even her mother had encouraged Rebecca to join the rest, all the while giving her a bright smile and, much to Rebecca's astonishment, a sly wink. This was, Rebecca realized, another opportunity for the gentlemen of the house to steal kisses from particular ladies, should they wish it. If any lady was discovered, then a forfeit must be offered and, given the fact that her last forfeit from Lord Burton had been only to dance with him, Rebecca was not certain what she could offer the next gentleman who found her. Her thoughts turned to Lord Hastings who, as yet, had not retrieved his forfeit from her. A delicate shiver ran over her skin as she thought about what it would be like to kiss him if that was, of course, the forfeit he required of her. Why had he not asked it from her as yet? What was it that made him linger so? Could it be that he had perhaps forgotten? That would not be very pleasing at all.

"Hush!"

Miss Moir's eyes opened wide as the sound of footsteps coming across the wooden floor reached both of their ears. Miss Moir was sitting on the windowsill in plain view of whoever it was that pulled back the drapes, whilst Rebecca was hiding to the side. There was every chance that Miss Moir would be discovered and that she would not, but perhaps, under the circumstances, Rebecca wanted that. A little solitude might do her the world of good, although, no doubt, her thoughts would be filled with one gentleman and one gentleman only.

"Ah-hah!"

With a great exclamation, the drapes were thrown back and the gentleman in question – one Lord Rosenthal bellowed Miss Moir's name. He did not, however, call Rebecca's name and thus it was Miss Moir who was hauled forward out onto the library floor, where she was taken along with Lord Rosenthal, laughing and giggling as she went. Rebecca closed her eyes and let out a slow breath as the door closed, finding herself rather astonished at how relieved she was that Lord Rosenthal had not found her.

"I have been waiting for Lord Rosenthal to find your friend."

Heat suddenly built in Rebecca as a voice she recognized tore through the drapes and towards her. Her heart pounded as a hand appeared, pulling back the drapes carefully, just as Lord Hastings came into view. For some moments, they looked into each other's eyes, only for Lord Hastings to laugh gruffly and shake his head.

"I must not allow myself to become distracted. Not this time," he murmured, coming to stand a little closer to her and, much to Rebecca's astonishment, pulling the drapes closed behind him. "There is much that we must talk of, and I have been seeking an opportunity where I can speak to you in private. But one look into your eyes and I am lost. Therefore, you will have to forgive me if I turn my gaze elsewhere."

A little surprised and overcome with the swell of emotion that was currently plaguing her heart, Rebecca let out a quiet laugh, which she quickly covered with her hand. Lord Hastings' eyes twinkled, and yet the truth of his words remained between them. He did not look away as he had said he would, and thus they continued to gaze into each other's faces, with Rebecca hardly knowing how she was taking in a breath, such was the furious pounding of her heart.

"I cannot tell you how much..." Taking a breath, Lord Hastings did not complete his sentence, but rather shook his head and let out a wry exclamation. "No, I shall not. Not at this moment at least." Taking a breath, he reached across and caught her hand. "The gentleman you saw, the one knocked from the horse, is now requesting to speak with you."

Rebecca's eyes widened, her stomach roiling. "He is still present, then? And has he told the Duke of his presence here? I have been eager to speak with you about him for some time, but there has never seemed to be an opportunity."

She watched as Lord Hastings pulled his eyebrows

together. "There is so much I must tell you, Lady Rebecca." So saying, he closed his eyes again and shook his head. "What you witnessed with the gentleman being pushed from his horse? That was all quite true, but the gentleman would say very little to me about the matter. I did not understand it – that is, not until I discovered who the second man was." Putting one hand to her heart, Rebecca stared long and hard at Lord Hastings, as though trying to decipher if he were telling her the truth. When he nodded, she drew in a sharp gasp, a sudden fear tumbling in her chest.

"Is he here? Is he one of the guests?"

Lord Hastings nodded slowly, reaching to grasp her hand. "He is now."

Uncertain as to what such a thing meant, it took Rebecca some moments to realize that he spoke of someone who had only just come in to the house, and after a few moments of consideration, realized it was none other than Mr. Shelbourne. For who else had arrived? There was no one else that had arrived recently. She stepped back sharply, her shoulder hitting the wall, and Lord Hastings quickly dropped her hand.

"I swear to you, I did not know." Holding up both hands for a moment, he dropped them back to his sides. "My brother has always been something of a difficulty. I have spent many years trying to curb his bad choices and to get him to consider his behavior more wisely, but he has always ignored me. I have not been able to keep his misdeeds hidden from all of society as I have wished, although I have been able to keep a good deal from them. Now, however, this course of action has made me so very concerned that I find myself uncertain what I ought to do. The gentleman in question will not speak to the Duke and has every intention of quitting the house and, thereafter, giving my brother what it is he has asked for. I have begged him not to do so and in return, he has stated that the only thing that will keep him here will be to speak with you first."

Taking a slow breath, Rebecca looked back at Lord Hastings for some moments. This was most extraordinary. The gentleman she had seen do such a dreadful thing was none other than Lord Hastings' brother. It was truly extraordinary to hear such a thing, although the more she considered it, the more Rebecca began to realize this was not as great a surprise as she first thought. After the man's behavior at the ball, she could not exactly call him an excellent fellow.

"I do not see what it is this man could gain from speaking with me?"

Lord Hastings dropped his gaze again so that it tumbled to the floor, his head dropping forward a little. "I believe he wants very much to discover whether you witnessed the entire incident. He wants to know precisely whether you will speak to the Duke on his behalf. No amount of assurances on my part that you would do so, and that you were honest also was enough to convince him. He wanted to speak with you and you alone. I can only pray he has not yet quit the house."

Rebecca licked her lips as she studied Lord Hastings. He continued to keep his head forward, his gaze dropped low. Did he truly think she would blame him for his brother's behavior? Or was it more that he was just embarrassed?

"You cannot believe I would think less of you because of your brother."

"No, perhaps not now, but I will admit it has always been my fear." One shoulder lifted when he still would not meet her gaze. "I have tried for many years to hide my brother's actions from as many people as I could. Do not think I have always been successful, for I know for certain I have not, but I have always had the concern that his actions would influence society's opinion of me. That is not to be unexpected, I suppose." Sending a quick glance towards her, he sighed heavily.

Rebecca reached out to touch his hand, seeing the light brown in his eyes slowly turn to darker brown. This was a part of him she had never seen before, for he had never unveiled it. He had never shown it to her, for in all the time they had spent together, she had not even known of his brother's foibles. Yes, she had been aware that he had a brother, although his name had not been mentioned, but it was that realization which had her shaking her head.

"I can well understand if you do not wish to linger in your acquaintance with me." Finally, Lord Hastings' gaze met hers. "If I am to lose your friendship twice, then at least the second time, it shall be your decision, and I will not hold it against you."

The horror of such a statement had her moving immediately forward. The space was small, and she had not anticipated just how close she would be to him. His breath was warm on her cheek as she looked up into his eyes, his gaze seeming to search her very own soul. She had not intended to be this close and yet now that she was here, now that her fingers were brushing across his hand, she found her free hand settling upon his chest. She did not want to be anywhere else.

"You are not your brother," she whispered softly. "That would be very wrong of me indeed, to hold you accountable for something your brother has done, no matter how dark it may be."

"But his influence on my family name cannot be

ignored. His behavior is no small matter and, as I have said, I am certain it will continue. It does not seem to matter how much I attempt to influence him. He is determined to tread his own dark path."

"You feel that heavy upon your soul?"

Lord Hastings hesitated, his hand going to settle over hers as it rested steadily against his heart. Rebecca paused, feeling it quicken and wondering at it. Did this mean that this brother of his had more of an influence on Lord Hastings' decisions than she had ever realized?

"Tell me something."

Lord Hastings' eyes closed briefly, as though he could barely look into her face for fear of what he would do if he lingered. "Anything."

Again, his heart quickened just a little under her hand and Rebecca allowed herself a small smile. "You said in your note that you wanted to tell me the truth... or as much of it as you could."

When Lord Hastings opened his eyes, he nodded but said nothing.

"I must wonder if your brother had any influence on our parting. You spoke to me of it once, but you never mentioned anything you have said today."

Lord Hastings offered her a wry smile, his hand still over hers. "That is not a question, Lady Rebecca, but if you are seeking to know whether my brother was involved in the ending of our closeness, then I will say that, indirectly, it was so." He sighed. "My brother was involved in a scheme at the time - a scheme that was most unfavorable. I confess I was afraid for you, afraid my connection with you would damage your reputation, should what my brother was doing be discovered. I did not want that."

Rebecca's eyes flared. "And is that why you wanted to

keep our connection a secret? You always said that such a thing was for a short while only, but you could not tell me why."

Lord Hastings nodded slowly, his gaze never leaving hers. "Perhaps it was not a fair decision, Rebecca, but I wanted to protect you. I did not want our connection to be made known for fear that my brother's nefarious schemes would be told to all of society - in which case, your connection to me could have damaged your reputation and I wanted to spare you from that. My intention was to make certain my brother could not continue with such wicked ways and thereafter, to ask your father for permission to court you."

Swallowing hard and a little surprised at the tears in her eyes that had come solely from him speaking the truth to her – the truth she had long wanted to hear – Rebecca took a moment to compose herself before she answered. "And I suppose you were not successful, given that we had to end our closeness?"

Lord Hastings did not answer immediately. Instead, something flashed in his eyes and his mouth pulled taut. Rebecca stared at him, her own heart pounding furiously. There was more to this matter, she realized. Yes, she had heard the truth – but only some of it. "Lord Hastings?"

His gaze pulled from hers. "I was successful in ending my brother's ploy." His shoulders dropped and Rebecca moved a little closer still, seeing how his eyes tumbled back to hers. Their hands were still pressed together, a fire seeming to light underneath them, sending billowing heat upwards. Her chin tipped as she leaned a little closer, seeing Lord Hastings' head lower. Her eyes closed, suddenly aware of just how desperately she wanted to be near to him... and precisely what that nearness should be.

The sound of the door opening had Rebecca tumbling back from Lord Hastings. Her shoulder hit the wall hard, and she winced, with Lord Hastings reaching out to steady her – just as Lord Rosenthal's loud voice echoed through the room again.

"I know you are here. I am certain that those drapes were open the last time I came into the room!"

With the very same dramatic gesture as he had used to discover Miss Moir, Lord Rosenthal threw back the drapes and exclaimed so loudly that Lord Hastings jumped. The smile of delight on Lord Rosenthal's face, however, quickly changed to one of surprise as he saw Rebecca standing there. His eyes twinkled and he immediately stepped back, dropping into an overly heavy bow.

"Pray forgive me. I did not mean to –"

"Alas, you have discovered me at the very moment I was to bring Lady Rebecca out from her hiding place," Lord Hastings chuckled, as Lord Rosenthal grinned. "You are not the only gentleman who was tasked with finding the ladies of the house, and I shall declare myself champion in this."

A flush rose in Rebecca's cheeks as Lord Hastings and Lord Rosenthal exchanged a look. She was glad to know Lord Rosenthal would not say anything to anyone, and that there was no danger of her reputation being damaged in any way, given that this was Christmas time and Christmas games were a plenty! Were this the summer season, then no doubt there would be a good many consequences for being discovered so, but for the moment, there would be none.

"I suppose you are to take her forfeit for yourself, then," Lord Rosenthal waggled his eyebrows, and Rebecca pressed both hands to her cheeks in embarrassment. Lord Hastings, however, grinned, turned and tipped his head to one side as he looked steadily at Rebecca.

"I shall not demand anything from the lady, but a kiss."

Rebecca turned wide eyes upon him, all the more astonished to hear him speak so openly. Was he intending to kiss her here, directly in front of Lord Rosenthal? She could not dream of such a thing, quite certain that her embarrassment would reach new heights should he dare do what he had suggested. Before she could even think of what to say, however, Lord Hastings had reached for her hand. Taking it, he lifted it to his mouth, pressed a gentle kiss to the back of her hand, pressed her fingers, and then released it.

A small smile crossed his lips. "And now I have taken my forfeit."

Lord Rosenthal's smile disappeared, and he threw up both hands. "You could have taken a much better forfeit than that," he protested, but Lord Hastings only shrugged, stepping forward from the window seat and turning towards Rebecca. She was sure her face had gone very red indeed, given that she could feel the heat burning in her cheeks, but her eyes were fixed on Lord Hastings, appreciating his understanding and consideration. His character, she told herself, appeared now to be an exceptional one. Just how much had she misjudged him?

"You shall be returned to the others who have been found. Although perhaps we might find time to play this game again at another time." Lord Hastings lifted one eyebrow, and immediately Rebecca understood what it was he was suggesting to her. Quickly, she moved closer to him and took his arm.

"I should be glad to," she replied softly. "And perhaps soon we will be able to find the time to have a conversation with that rather quiet gentleman you spoke of. I should like that very much."

"No quiet gentlemen as far as I can see," Lord Rosenthal laughed, but Lord Hastings smiled at once, a light forming in his eyes. It was a memory of the gentleman she had once known – the gentleman who had promised her so much, had hoped for so much, and to whom her heart still belonged.

CHAPTER TEN

Myles was relieved to return to the servant's bedchamber and find Lord Richards still present. A large part of him had been afraid he would step inside, only to find it vacant, but to see Lord Richards sitting there, a book in hand, had been an overwhelming relief. His promise that Lady Rebecca would come to speak to him as soon as she was able had been met with a small smile and Myles had sworn that it was only a matter of when she would be able to slip away. Lord Richards had stated that he had no intention of leaving and thus, Myles' concern had been somewhat relieved. Thus far, however, it had been one full day since he had spoken to Lord Richards and still, that time had not yet come.

Perhaps we shall have an opportunity later this afternoon, once the ladies have returned from their walk in the grounds.

Shrugging inwardly to himself, he gazed down at the whisky in his glass, swirling it around and paying very little attention to anything else going on in the drawing room. It had been a quieter day and Myles was grateful for the chance to rest.

"This is an excellent house party, I must say. I have been very grateful for your hospitality, Your Grace."

Myles started in surprised upon hearing his brother's voice. He had managed to ignore Shelbourne's chatter on the whole, but there seemed to be no doing so now. The man was determined to speak, determined to make himself known and, Myles considered, no doubt he had the intention of using his connection with these gentlemen to his own advantage at some point in the future. Myles scowled. The less time his brother was here, the better.

"Not at all." The Duke waved a hand, his voice slurring a little – no doubt from the great amount of port he had already imbibed that evening, and this was before they had even gone through to sit with the ladies! There was to be Christmas entertainment also, a festive play that Myles was sure he would enjoy – so long as he could sit close to Lady Rebecca.

"Tell me, Your Grace," Shelbourne continued. "Have all of your guests arrived?"

The Duke blinked slowly, obviously a little confused by the question, as Myles also sat up a little straighter. Whatever was his brother doing in asking such a thing? Perhaps he had chosen to do so now, when the Duke was a little befuddled, for it would be more likely that the Duke would answer. The other gentlemen were involved in the quieter conversations, but Myles paid close attention to his brother, silently trying to figure out what such a question could mean and where his brother was intending to lead the conversation.

"There are one or two absent, I suppose," the Duke shrugged. "I do not mind particularly for, as most gentlemen here know, I was less than eager to have such a house party. It was my mother who determined that it should be so. However, now that we are in the midst of it, I will say that my enjoyment has increased significantly." A lopsided smile caught one side of his mouth and Myles noticed it immediately, wondering what it was specifically – or who it was – that had caused the Duke of Meyrick to smile so. His attention was drawn again quickly to his brother as Shelbourne continued to speak, asking yet more prying questions.

"I think it very rude indeed that certain people would not turn up to your house party, particularly if they have been invited. That is very ill mannered, do you not think? Who are these gentlemen that would do such a thing as that?" He shook his head, his jaw tight. "I should like to know their names so that I do not permit myself a close acquaintance with them, given how they have been so rude to Your Grace."

In that one moment, Myles knew exactly what it was his brother was doing. He was seeking to discover whether Lord Richards was present somewhere in the house or if he were gone elsewhere. After all, Myles considered, his brother's supposition was well founded, for if the gentleman had been badly injured, as Shelbourne assumed, then the only place that he might have been taken was the Duke's manor. Myles recalled also how Lord Richards had stated that Shelbourne must have known, one way or the other, that he had been invited to the Duke's Christmas house party. There was little doubt that his brother was now wondering where Lord Richards had gone. Thus, in speaking to the Duke as he did, he was attempting to discover the man's whereabouts. After all, there had been no astonishing news that an injured gentleman had been found on the estate, but clearly, Shelbourne's suspicion was that the viscount was somewhere here.

I am now, in fact, a little relieved that Lord Richards has chosen to stay in the servants' quarters, and that he begged me to keep his presence from the Duke!

Letting out a slow breath, Myles shot a hard look to his brother, but Shelbourne was looking steadily at the Duke. None of this came as a surprise. He had been certain that his brother had come here for a reason, and this was exactly as he had expected from someone such as he.

"Do you not think it is time for us to take our leave, Your Grace? The ladies will be waiting."

His attempt to distract the Duke was foiled by the Duke himself, however, for the man immediately waved a hand, dismissing the statement.

"I am certain that the ladies will enjoy their tea and will have not noticed the absence of our company as yet," he answered. Shelbourne chuckled, clearly aware by his sneering grin that Myles had been foiled. "Besides which, the actors are not yet ready for us. Once they are, we shall join the ladies and you shall again be with your particular lady – whichever one is your favorite at present!"

The other gentlemen guffawed and Myles had to force a smile, pretending that he found the remark mirthful. The other gentlemen immediately talked amongst themselves about who had stolen various kisses and embraces from whom, but Myles kept his full attention on Shelbourne.

"Your Grace?"

The innocent expression on Shelbourne's face brought a glaring anger to Myles, but he clamped his mouth shut. All he could do at present was listen.

"Yes?" The Duke frowned, then his expression cleared as he recalled the question Shelbourne had already set him.

"Ah, yes. In regards to those who are not present, there is one Lord Brookmire who has not arrived, and whilst there will be a reason for this at some point, it is not as though I expected him to arrive." He chuckled and shook his head. "He is very often absent without explanation."

"And the other?" Shelbourne asked as Myles shook his head in frustration, wishing he could find a way to distract the Duke. "Who else is absent?"

The Duke of Meyrick considered, then shrugged both shoulders. "There is one other, but I cannot recall his name. Such a thing does not matter, I suppose, since you have arrived here, Shelbourne, and can take his place!"

At this, Shelbourne opened his mouth to say something more, but Myles immediately intercepted him by rising to his feet. He could not say anything overt as regarded his brother, could not state his concerns aloud over Shelbourne's intentions but neither could he allow his brother to say anything further, for, in order to protect Lord Richards, the conversation had to be drawn to a close. This was intolerable from his brother. Myles simply could not allow it to continue.

"Is there a reason you are asking so many questions, brother?" Meandering towards his brother, he lifted an eyebrow. "Was there someone here you expected to be present? Was that the reason for your arrival, and are you now facing grave disappointment over their absence?"

His brother's smile faded quickly as he looked from one gentleman to the other whilst at the same time rising from the table. The fact that Myles had already stood up had garnered a good deal of attention from the other gentlemen and, from the way his eyes snapped around the room, Shelbourne was all too aware of it.

"No, there is not," he snapped, his sharp tongue

catching yet more attention from the other gentlemen. "That is a foolish question. I happened upon this house quite by accident and I am grateful for the Duke's hospitality. I only thought to make certain that there was nothing.... unscrupulous, taking place at present. I should not like to acquaint myself with any gentleman who has treated the Duke without the appropriate consideration!"

"I understand." Rising from the table – albeit with a little difficulty, the Duke of Meyrick made his way to the door. The other gentlemen, seeing the Duke about to quit the room, immediately followed suit. "Come now, gentlemen, Lord Hastings is quite right. We do not want to leave the ladies waiting for us for too long and there is the Christmas play to soon enjoy!"

Myles smiled to himself as his brother glared at him. The Duke made for the door, only to turn around and make his way back towards Shelbourne. Myles watched in amused relief as the Duke slapped Shelbourne hard on the back, making the man stumble forward.

"You have excellent intentions, I am sure, but there is no need for such concern. I am a Duke, am I not? If there is anything unscrupulous, I am already aware of it, I assure you. There are no secrets kept from me! And any gentlemen who treat my invitations with a complete lack of consideration will be made fully aware of their failure in my eyes, have no doubt." Again, the Duke laughed and this time, the other gentleman in the room joined him.

"But of course."

Shelbourne managed a smile, but Myles saw the ice behind his eyes. The smile faded from his expression as the group meandered to the door, intending to make their way to the drawing room instead. Perhaps his brother was not the only one who had been foolish. After what the Duke of

Meyrick had said, could he still believe the Duke was entirely unaware of Lord Richards' presence here? After all, the man's horse was in stables and even though the Duke's staff had promised to remain silent, that did not mean that they had done so. Their duty was to the Duke, not to either Myles or Lord Richards.

"You understand, then?" The Duke's voice echoed down the hallway, floating back towards Myles and Shelbourne as they made their way through the dining room door. "You need not be concerned, not in any way."

"Of course you are right. My concerns are for naught." Shelbourne smiled quickly in case anyone should look, only to turn his head and throw a glare towards Myles, which he accepted with only a shrug. He did not care whether his interference frustrated his brother for, as far as he was concerned, it was merited. His heart remained troubled, however, as he continued from the room. The first concern was what exactly his brother had intended to do by asking so many questions, with the second making him wonder whether the Duke knew that Lord Richards resided here already. Had he deliberately forgotten Lord Richards' name, choosing not to give it to Shelbourne?

"I must wonder why you are so concerned about interrupting my questions to the Duke."

Myles glanced at his brother who had held back from the others so he might fall into step with him.

"And I must wonder at your intentions in asking him so many things," Myles replied quietly. "There is always a reason with you, brother – usually an immoral reason, I might add. I do not trust you, and I do not want the Duke of Meyrick to trust you, either." His brother set one hand to his heart, pretending to be greatly upset, no doubt.

"How could you say such a thing to me?"

Myles shook his head and then turned away. He did not believe his brother's expressions, not even for a moment.

"You realize what you have done, do you not?" Undeterred, his brother's voice reached Myles' ears again. "You have made quite certain that I shall continue to linger on in interest, wondering why it is you have pushed me so far from asking those particular questions. There *must* be a reason for it, and I am determined to find out what that reason is."

Hearing truth in his brother's words and feeling his heart jump with sudden concern, Myles swiveled his head towards Shelbourne. "Whatever is it you think you have learned? What is it you think you can gain from me? You will be disappointed, I can assure you. There is nothing of any purpose in my determinations, other than to keep you from the Duke." The lies came quickly, suddenly afraid that he had spoken thoughtlessly. He had not given a moment's consideration as to what his brother would think of his interference.

"I do not believe you."

Rounding on his brother, he put out one arm, and Shelbourne was forced to come to stop.

"Understand this, Shelbourne." He spoke as calmly as he could, but his eyes narrowed all the same. "I know you. I may not understand your specific intentions, but I am certain that they are dark. Whatever it is you intend to do, I am quite certain that it cannot be good. You say you are here quite by accident, but I will not believe you, and I will continue to push you away from the Duke of Meyrick. I will continue to prevent you from asking leading questions that will, no doubt, aid you in whatever scheme it is you have planned. I will make myself perfectly clear, Shelbourne – I want you to leave this place having no success whatsoever, and I want to make certain that the Duke of Meyrick *himself* is protected, without bringing a stain to our family name. The name you so carelessly tread on every time you concoct something all the more vile." He spoke firmly but his brother's eyes only searched his without saying a single utterance and for what felt like an age, they simply looked into one another's faces.

Then his brother laughed horribly, spat a few choice words at Myles, and then hurried to join the others, leaving Myles breathing heavily and staring after his brother. There was no doubt in his mind that everything he had just said was simply falling on deaf ears. His brother did not care about his own reputation, never mind the reputation of his family name and the title Myles bore – and the responsibility to protect it once more settled over Myles' shoulders. It seemed, to his mind, his brother did not believe that Myles had spoken without intention and he cursed himself silently for speaking so openly without thought.

Now, his brother would be the one watching him.

∽

"So begins a winter's tale." The Christmas play was in progress when Lord Hastings returned to the room.

Pressing his lips together and taking in short breaths so as to rid himself of any remaining tension, Myles made his way towards Lady Rebecca, coming to sit on the left side of her, nearest to the wall. The room was rather dark, and the players were at the very front of the room. The fire was their backdrop and there were many candles on either side, but further back into the room, all the candles had been doused, which was very much to Myles' advantage.

Lady Rebecca glanced at him, and then her smile

quickly spread across her face. "You have come to sit with me, Lord Hastings?"

Reaching across, he pressed her hand for a moment. "I come to steal you away, Lady Rebecca."

Twisting her head sharply, her eyes went wide, her cheeks coloring furiously.

"We must go and see Lord Richards – and this is the only time when I think we will not be missed." Not wanting her to have any false idea as to why he wanted her company at this very moment, right when the Christmas play was about to begin, Myles quickly made himself clear. "If we do not go now, then I fear my brother will note us missing later on. He has every intention of paying very close attention to me, and I believe it is only now that we will have opportunity to slip away. I will be watched with a careful eye otherwise."

Lady Rebecca's eyes remained a little wide, but after a moment, she nodded. "What is it you want me to do?"

Myles cast a glance over his shoulder. There was no one behind him. His brother was sitting very close to the front, next to a beautiful and very wealthy young woman. No doubt he was wondering how he might use her to his own advantage.

"I shall take my leave. I will wait for you in the parlor. If you are able to absent yourself for a short while, then pray, come and find me. We will go to the bedchamber together to speak to the viscount and thereafter, return here, one after the other. I know there is a great risk in doing so, and certainly your reputation could be in danger if we are discovered, but –"

"That means very little to me." Lady Rebecca's fingers touched his lightly, and she gave him a small smile. "I will take my leave in a few minutes. I do not think I will be noticed, but if I am, I will come up with some excuse"

He held her gaze. "I thank you,"

With quick strides but silent feet, he made his way across the room. Reaching the door, he grasped the handle, then turned his head, suddenly afraid that his brother would look straight at him. It took him a moment to make everyone out, but with relief he saw his brother was still facing straight ahead, looking at the players rather than behind him. Praying it would remain so, Myles turned and, opening the door as slowly and as quietly as he could, stepped out into the hallway. Choosing to leave the door a little ajar, he walked slowly, alone along the hallway and back towards the parlor. His stomach knotted uncomfortably as he considered all that he had asked Lady Rebecca to do. She was taking a great risk and, in joining him, would have to be very cautious indeed that she was not discovered by anyone. If there was even a question over what they were doing together out in the Duke's house without a single soul for company – when there was no Christmas parlor game taking place – then Myles knew what would be expected. No doubt it would cause great consternation, and after what had happened before, where he had been pushed away from Lady Rebecca, he did not want such a thing to happen. He would take a great care to protect her so that there would not be even a question over her reputation. Yes, it was Christmas time and certainly all expectations of propriety were little changed, but that did not mean he didn't have a responsibility to her as well as to himself.

Swallowing against a tightness that had grown slowly in his chest as he thought of her, Myles made his way to the parlor and, pushing open the door, stepped inside. It was empty and after a moment he dropped into a chair, letting out a great and heavy sigh. His hand pressed to his forehead, his elbow into the arm of the chair. The heaviness of his responsibility was weighing down upon him, making him feel as though he were sinking into the floor. He could only pray he would soon find relief, that Lord Richards would be willing to speak with both Lady Rebecca and, thereafter with the Duke of Meyrick. That way he could bring an end to all of this difficulty, for his brother would be shamed in front of a great and officious Duke, and, Myles prayed, would not dare to show himself to the Duke or to any of his acquaintances again.

"I might find myself a little free." Mumbling to himself, Myles' heart lifted in his chest as he considered what it would be like *not* to have to consider his brother. That freedom would be both unknown and deeply appreciated, for he would no longer have to worry about what Shelbourne was doing.

But there was a caveat to that. If they proceeded with this plan, then there was every chance that his brother's misdeeds would be made known to practically all of England. He would not be able to hide from it and the shame he had been avoiding for so long would be suddenly cast all over him. What of Lady Rebecca? What of the closeness they had begun to discover again? It was not as though he would be able to court her, should such a thing take place.

Yet, I cannot push her from my mind.... nor my heart.

A sad smile spread across his face as he dropped his hand and pushed his head back against the chair. He had long thought of Lady Rebecca and even though he had been forced to step back from her, his feelings had never changed. That was why he had found his heart so pained, he realized. It was because he simply could not forget his feelings for her. He had come to care for her so very deeply. A little uncertain as to what it was like to be in love with someone, Myles had to admit that such a great swell of emotion had never been brought about in him before. He had not even known himself capable of feeling such things and yet, that had all come about because of his nearness again to Lady Rebecca. He did not want to leave her behind, had never wanted to return to his seat and leave her in London, but he had been given very little choice. But Christmas, it seemed, had pushed them back together. What was he to do?

"What if she asks me about why we had to separate? Will I tell her the truth?" It had always been in his mind to explain to her about his brother and how his behavior had led to so much shame, but that in itself had not been the only reason he had separated himself from her - and he was all too aware that Lady Rebecca understood that. If she asked him for the truth, then would he have the strength to keep it from her, as he had done before? He did not want to cause her more pain. To prove that he was a gentleman, even if he had been unfairly treated, meant keeping one part of the whole situation to himself. But could he do it?

His questions flew from his head as the door opened, and as he hurried himself out of the chair, Lady Rebecca stood framed in the doorway. They simply looked at each other for a long moment, neither saying a word. And then, before Myles understood what was happening, she had crossed the room and had flung herself into his arms.

Myles sucked in air, finding himself overwhelmed by the strength of feeling that was brought to him by her actions. His arms went about her waist, and he held her close so that her head rested on his shoulder. Why had he ever let this beautiful, wondrous creature part from him?

Why had he allowed himself to be so bullied, to be so influenced? Perhaps he ought to have been truthful with Lady Rebecca from the very beginning, but given how much it would pain her, Myles knew he could never have done so... and could not do so now. He could tell her of his heart, certainly, could tell her the truth behind his situation back in the summer Season as regarded his brother – but the reason for their separation could never be told. Not unless he received express permission to do so.

"We- we should go."

When Lady Rebecca looked up at him, a small sigh escaping from her, Myles smiled down into her face, raising one hand so that it might brush lightly across her cheek. "Do not misunderstand me, I should very much like to remain here and hold you close for some time, but every moment is precious." Unwillingly, his hand fell to his side, and he silently demanded that he step back. "But once this matter is at a close, there is a good deal more that we must say to each other, I think."

She smiled at him then, her face a delicate pink as her eyes fastened themselves to his. "There certainly is a great deal to say, yes," she admitted quietly, another sigh breaking from her lips. "Would that we could stay here! But for the moment, we should depart. Lead the way, Lord Hastings and I will follow you."

CHAPTER ELEVEN

"I believe the gentleman is uncertain of me still."

A little confused, Rebecca looked up at Lord Hastings as they made their way towards the bedchamber where Lord Richards resided. "I do not understand. Why should he be unsure of you?"

"Because he has learned that I am Shelbourne's brother. He does not trust my brother, so why should he trust me?" Lord Hastings gave her a wry smile. "I do not blame him. After all he has endured, it is more than understandable."

Rebecca nodded slowly, her lips pursing gently as they continued to make their way down the servants' staircase. Perhaps, she considered, this was why Lord Richards had wanted to meet with her. He had wanted to make certain that Lord Hastings was exactly as he seemed. *I will be able to reassure him,* she thought to herself. *I know Lord Hastings is of excellent character, even though I believed quite the opposite for some time.*

A twist of nerves ran around her stomach as she made her way into the small bedchamber, being entirely unsure what to expect. A little surprised to see a gentleman rise easily from his chair to greet her, she recalled thereafter that Lord Hastings had stated Lord Richards was not severely injured – but even then, she had not expected him to be so well recovered.

"As promised." Turning, Lord Hastings put one hand around her waist and led her in. "My Lord Richards, might I present Lady Rebecca."

The gentleman bowed towards her, but Rebecca did not miss the slight wince that came as he lifted his head. Evidently, he was still in a little pain.

"Good evening, Lord Richards. I am pleased to make your acquaintance. I am also very relieved to hear you were not severely injured after what took place. It is good to see you standing again."

The gentleman studied her for some moments, giving her a small smile. "Lord Hastings tells me you are the one who witnessed what happened to me. Is that so?"

She nodded. "Yes, that is so. I saw everything. I was not seen, however, and I did watch from a distance, which is why I did not recognize Mr. Shelbourne when he came to join the house party."

The man bit his lip and turned away, a slight frown furrowing his forehead. Glancing at Lord Hastings and seeing him lift a shoulder, Rebecca took a breath and stepped forward a little more.

"Lord Richards, might I be so bold as to state that I understand your present dilemma? You feel as though you will need to give in to all Mr. Shelbourne demands of you, simply to prevent such a thing from happening again. The injury you sustained was not insignificant, I understand – and your fear is now that, should you refuse to do as he asks, he will injure you all the more severely."

Lord Richards turned to her, the lines on his forehead marking deeper still, but Rebecca did not hesitate.

"Regardless of this, my concern is that if you do such a thing as that, then Mr. Shelbourne will be able to continue on with such behavior. Strength is required to stand up against him."

Lord Richards shook his head. "You state it would require strength, but it does not seem to me as though that is the only thing needed." Taking a breath, he looked at Lord Hastings. "Your brother will need to be shown that such behaviors, such wickedness as he has placed on myself and, no doubt, on others, cannot happen again. He must be shown that his actions are unacceptable, will not be allowed to continue, and will not be tolerated." Flinging out one hand towards Lord Hastings, he shook his head. "And I believe you have already tried on multiple occasions, Lord Hastings."

Lord Hastings cleared his throat and when he spoke, his voice was gruff. "Yes, Lord Richards. That is so."

"Well then." Shrugging, Lord Richards turned his back on them both and, once more, took a seat by the fire. "Given that his own brother has been unable to stop Mr. Shelbourne from such a course of action, then how can I have any hope of success? Given that I am only an acquaintance of Mr. Shelbourne – and someone he has already taken advantage of?"

Unable to answer that question, Rebecca looked across at Lord Hastings, but he was looking down at the floor, his hand running over his chin. This did not fill Rebecca with any sort of hope. Silence flooded the room for some moments until, much to Rebecca's relief, Lord Hastings began to speak.

"I will tell you the difference, Lord Richards." Taking a breath, Lord Hastings lifted his head. "This time, it will not only be myself speaking with my brother. *That* will have an influence." Speaking slowly, he took a few steps forward towards the gentleman. "Thus far, I have been trying to keep my brother's actions hidden to protect the reputation of my title and have never involved anyone else. That will change. Do not throw aside the Duke's influence. If we tell him what has taken place, and I am honest about what the difficulties with Shelbourne have been ever since I have taken on the title, then my brother will not be able to simply continue on as he has been."

"And that is why you wished to speak with me also, was it not?" Rebecca added softly. "You wanted to make certain I would speak up on your behalf, to verify it all, and I can assure you that I will. I will tell the Duke everything I saw. He will know exactly what it was Shelbourne sought to do to you and, with his brother speaking against him also, there can be nothing for you to fear."

"You saw me fall." Lord Richards looked at her and then closed his eyes. "I confess I do not recall what happened afterwards, but Lord Hastings has told me of it." The man shuddered, and Rebecca immediately took a step forward, one hand going to his shoulder, her sympathy rising furiously.

"I am sorry for what took place. I saw the dreadful actions Mr. Shelbourne took and I am only sorry I did not go to you immediately. I should have done but fear kept me back until he was gone."

She dropped her hand, but Lord Richards caught it briefly, turning his head so he might hold her gaze. "You were courageous, Lady Rebecca. If it were not for you, I would have been all the more injured, I am sure of it." Sighing heavily, he dropped her hand. "But you do not know what this man can do. He has already tried to injure me most severely, simply because I would not pay him what he stated I owed. I know it was a lie, but his threats are such that I am afraid for those I love."

"But you know my brother," Lord Hastings replied quietly. "Understand that I have done all I can. I have removed as much as I can from him – including his financial wealth – and that, no doubt, is why he has chosen to swindle others to gain coin. Just because he has done such a thing to you once does not mean he will not do such a thing again."

"Indeed, if you have given in to his threats this time, then will he not think himself quite able to demand even more from you the second time?" Seeing the fear in the man's eyes still, Rebecca reached out one hand to his shoulder again, recalling what Lord Hastings had said as they had made their way towards the bedchamber.

"Be assured Lord Hastings is an excellent gentleman. Has no desire for further injury to come to you. When he speaks of his brother's cruel spirit, his word is true. It has injured him a great deal also, just as it has injured you, albeit in a different fashion. His eagerness to end such cruelty comes from his heart. You can trust him, Lord Richards." Turning her head, she looked over at Lord Hastings, a gentle smile gracing her lips. "Just as I do." She spoke honestly, with every word coming from her heart. Lord Hastings smiled, and Rebecca could not look away from him. Such was the roar of emotion swelling within her heart. Everything she had felt for Lord Hastings at one time had come back, but with an even greater strength. She did not think she would ever be free of it and yet, that awareness seemed to fill her with a great and overwhelming joy. She *wanted* these feelings to linger, even to grow. Yes, there was still something of a mystery as regarded his absence from her back in London, but she was quite certain the cause of it had a great deal to do with his brother.

"You honor me with your trust."

"I give it freely," she answered softly, as if Lord Richards was not in the room. "It may have gone from me for a time, but I see now there was more to your parting than I thought. It was not merely a change of heart, but rather, there was something of significance that forced us asunder – which I now know was partly to do with your brother, although you have not told me all of it as yet. But even if you choose not to do so, even if I am to never find out the entire truth, I will still hold you in my mind as a greatly esteemed gentleman who ought to be highly respected and admired." She choked with emotion and to gain control, she turned back to Lord Richards before she lost her train of thought. "I assure you, Lord Richards, that in speaking with the Duke, with both myself and Lord Hastings by your side, the matter with Mr. Shelbourne will be brought to a swift conclusion. The Duke of Meyrick has a great deal of influence. Once Mr. Shelbourne's wrongdoing is made known to the Duke, I have no cause to doubt he will do everything in his power to protect both you and others from him."

Lord Richards rubbed one hand over his eyes, suddenly appearing very weary indeed. "But in doing such a thing, Lord Hastings, do you not risk that very thing you have been trying so hard to protect?"

Rebecca glanced at Lord Hastings, then looked towards Lord Richards again. He was right, she realized, a sudden cold chill running down her spine. If the Duke of Meyrick decided that all the guests here at this house party needed to know of Mr. Shelbourne wrongdoings, then such news would, no doubt, spread through all of society – throughout all of England, in fact. And that meant his attempt to protect his family name, the very thing Lord Hastings had been doing his best to keep secure, might well be in danger of ruination.

Much to Rebecca's astonishment, when she looked back at Lord Hastings, there was a small smile on his face as he pushed out both hands gently. "Perhaps I have been wrong in attempting to protect my title from every little scrutiny," he said quietly. "My brother is wicked, selfish, cruel and greedy, but I never once imagined he would attempt to kill another fellow simply because of some scheme to take a few coins. I did not think he would *ever* go to such lengths and now, I think it is time to accept the fact that my family name *will* have a shadow cast over it. I can do nothing to protect it from that, for it is my brother's doing. I must only hope that if such a thing does occur, that society would look upon me graciously, blaming my brother rather than myself.... although I am not certain every single person in our set would be of such a mind!"

Catching her lip between her teeth, Rebecca considered this statement, saw the truth of it, and found herself frowning. Yes, she realized, yes, many in society would link both Lord Hastings and his brother together, believing them to be of the same ilk, even though Lord Hastings had done nothing wrong. Some would turn their back on him, some would give him the cut direct, and some would come in search of recompense for what his brother had done. Her heart ached with a sudden pain as though she were standing alongside Lord Hastings and his dilemma. How much she longed to take that burden from him and yet, as she looked back at him again, she saw his shoulders drop as the smile lingered on his lips.

It appeared as though Lord Hastings was quite accepting of the situation.

"What do you say then, Lord Richards?"

Both she and Lord Hastings waited as the gentleman stood up and began to pace up and down the room. He muttered to himself occasionally, and he walked for some minutes, clearly thinking about what they had suggested and going over in his mind what he had planned. Rebecca grew rather impatient, a little afraid that her absence from the play would be noticed. What would her mother say if she were discovered in the hall, alone, with Lord Hastings? Licking her lips, she clasped her hands in front of her. Tightening her fingers. Releasing them up again and again as Lord Richards continued to consider.

Suddenly, he spun on his heel, planted his feet, lifted his chin and placed his hands at his waist. "Yes, I shall do it."

His strong stance was a little hindered by the slight quiver in his voice, but Rebecca found herself beaming as Lord Hastings strode forward to slap the gentleman on the shoulder.

"Capital, capital! You have made the right decision, Lord Richards. And I'll arrange a meeting with both the Duke and my brother. For tomorrow, if I can. I will not permit my brother to know of the reason for such a meeting. We must make sure he is surprised by it, else I fear he will not tell us anything."

Rebecca, quite frankly, wanted to hug the gentleman, but chose instead simply to press Lord Richards' hand for a moment without saying a word. He smiled back at her – the first smile that had ever crossed his face, and suddenly he seemed a good deal younger than he had ever appeared before.

"And you shall be there also, Lady Rebecca?"

"Of course I shall be. You have my word." Making her way to the door, she waited for Lord Hastings, who said a few things more to Lord Richards before coming to join her. With a quick smile towards Lord Richards, Rebecca quit the room and immediately hurried along to the staircase. Neither of them spoke until they reached the hall that would lead them back to the drawing room.

"You have succeeded, Lady Rebecca."

The gentle press of Lord Hastings' hand on her shoulder had Rebecca almost desperate to leap into his arms, and indeed she almost stopped, stumbling a little as she turned to look at him. Lord Hastings was smiling broadly, and her heart flew up within her, delighted to see the smile that now lingered on his face. When had she last seen him smile in such a way? It had not been for some months and how glad she was now to see it upon his features again.

"I would stop to embrace you, Lady Rebecca, but I fear that if I were to do so, we should never return to the drawing room!" So saying, Lord Hastings reached and caught her hand so that they were connected to each other as they walked back along the hall. "I am very well aware there is still more that needs to be shared between us, but for the moment, I *have* to return you to the drawing room before the play is at an end and we are discovered."

"And would that be so very bad a thing?"

Astonished at her own question, Rebecca came to a sudden stop, just as Lord Hastings turned to face her, his eyes wide, his jaw a little slack as she looked up into his face, her heart beating furiously as though it were a bird trapped in a cage, desperate to be set free.

"I do not think it would be," she whispered as he drew

nearer. A sudden, desperate urge to be closer to him than she had ever been before burned in her heart. Her hand went to his shoulder while his settled on her waist – and then the sound of a door opening and closing had them stumbling back.

Before she knew what was happening, Rebecca was pulled back into another room. The door was pushed closed and Lord Hastings stood beside it, looking through the small gap as the footsteps drew nearer. Rebecca pushed herself a little closer to the wall, her hands going to her mouth as though she could hide her breath from whoever it was walking down the hallway. It certainly was not her mother, for the footsteps were much too strong and sharp to be her mother's soft slippers. Nor could it be Lady Meyrick, for again her slippers would make very little noise on the floor. To her mind, the steps sounded like those of a gentleman, and in an instant, she knew exactly why Lord Hastings had pulled her away so quickly.

She closed her eyes as the footsteps drew nearer, only to let her breath out slowly as they thereafter began to retreat, walking past the door that hid them both. Lord Hastings let out a slow breath before turning to her.

"Are you quite all right, Lady Rebecca?"

She nodded and came closer to him. "Who was that gentleman?"

Lord Hastings shook his head and, by the grim expression on his face, Rebecca already knew who it was that had come searching for them both.

It had been none other than Shelbourne.

CHAPTER TWELVE

"Mama, I must speak with you."

Her mother looked up, seeming a little surprised to hear Rebecca speak so sharply. The small parlor was almost vacant save for the two of them, but Rebecca found herself increasingly nervous as she waited for her meeting with the Duke to take place.

"What is it, my dear?"

A little encouraged by her own tenacity, Rebecca drew in a breath. "It is about Lord Hastings."

Her mother immediately set her book in her lap, closing it completely before her hands settled on top of it. Her brows lifted, but she did not say a single thing, clearly waiting for Rebecca to continue.

"I must know why father does not wish me to be closely acquainted with him. There must be a reason why I am being discouraged from having a close connection. That reason has never been explained to me."

"That is because we did not think there was any need to explain it to you, my dear," her mother answered softly. "There was never a connection between you two."

"That is because there could not be, even if I had wanted it," Rebecca replied, a little more sharply than she had intended. "If I had begun to favor Lord Hastings, Father would have told me that I was not permitted to do so, just as you yourself have stated this very week. I am curious as to why."

Her mother's expression did not change. "And is there some reason you are asking me this question now, Rebecca?"

Rebecca turned her gaze away. "There may well be, but that is not the point. I should like to know what cause there is for such a thing to be required of me."

Her mother sighed and shook her head. "My dear girl, you cannot have your head turned by a gentleman just because he has stolen a kiss or two as a forfeit."

"That is not what I – nor he – has done!" Turning sharply to face her mother, Rebecca flung up one hand in a gesture of frustration. "Is it not possible for me to become enamored with a particular gentleman? I find his character *more* than acceptable and I should like to know what exactly it is that is keeping me from pursuing a closer connection with him."

Lady Wilbram tutted lightly. "Rebecca, listen to me. It does not matter what you want. Lord Hastings will never consider you as more than an acquaintance. You can be assured of that."

It was as though someone had pushed Rebecca so hard that she stumbled. Her heart leaped out of her chest with fright as the realization as to what must have occurred suddenly took a hold of her. Taking in gasping breaths, she saw her mother eyes narrowing slightly, worry written into the lines on her forehead. But she could hear nothing apart from the quickened beat of her heart. Surely it could not be? Surely it had not been her father who had told Lord Hastings to remove his connection from Rebecca? Had he been forced into a course of action that he did not want to take?

Her eyes closed.

There is so much of this matter that I do not yet fully understand.

"There are plenty of other excellent gentlemen," her mother continued, as though what she had said was of very little consequence. "This is precisely what the Christmas season – and such house parties – can do to a young woman. One can feel a strong interest for a gentleman given the affections that are offered, but you must not allow your heart to become at all affected. It will pass quickly enough."

"And what if that is something that I do not wish for?" Rebecca quickly returned. "What if I do not want my feelings to pass? I have already made up my mind, Mama. Unless you or Father can give me specific reason as to why Lord Hastings is not to be considered, I can assure you that he is the only one I am thinking of at present – and shall be for some time."

To Rebecca's very great upset, however, her mother did not seem to accept this. She simply trilled a laugh, as though Rebecca was being quite ridiculous.

"La, you have only had too many kisses under the mistletoe," she replied with a wave of her hand. "That is all this is – and bear in mind, you have not had such an experience before and therefore, I can understand your desire for such feelings to grow. But I can assure you, my dear girl, they will fade, and they will fade quickly. It is Christmas time. It is a house party. It is quite reasonable for you to have all manner of emotions, but I can assure you that they are not at all significant. They will disappear quickly indeed once you are at home again."

Rebecca was about to open her mouth to reject all her mother had said, but after a moment, she chose not to do so. Regardless of what her mother thought, she was quite determined in her own mind. She was not about to lose what she had built again with Lord Hastings, for her feelings were much too significant for that now. Whatever her father's reasons for keeping her back from him, it would not be enough to hold her back.

"Come now. You need not look so disappointed. Recall that I was young once also, and I understand all that you are experiencing. You will not like that I have said that your feelings will fade quickly, but that is the truth, my dear, and it would not be fair of me to hold that back from you."

Placing a cool smile to her lips, Rebecca made to sit down quietly, only for the door to open and Miss Moir to step in. Her eyes were a little rounded, but she looked straight at Rebecca rather than at her mother and instantly Rebecca knew the time had come.

"Lady Rebecca, sh - should you like to walk with me for a time?" Miss Moir asked, shooting a sideways glance at Lady Wilbram. "We need not go outdoors, but perhaps we could take a walk around the manor house itself or make our way to the library where some of the other young ladies are. I believe they are making Christmas decorations for the Duke's house and would be glad of our help."

"Certainly I would be glad to." Rising from her chair, she walked to her friend without so much as a backward glance towards her mother. Quitting the room, she let out a long breath, glad to now be free of her mother's presence for a short while at least.

"Is everything ready?"

Miss Moir nodded, her eyes still wide. "I do not understand entirely what is going on. The Duke and Lord Hastings are in his study and the Duke of Meyrick has requested your presence. I am to come with you also. I hope that is quite all right."

"That is more than all right. Thank you very much for being so willing, my dear friend. I know you do not understand all but it will all be clear soon enough. One thing I shall tell you is this will be the moment Mr. Shelbourne learns he cannot behave in such a fashion any longer."

Miss Moir shook her head. "He is an unseemly sort, then?"

Rebecca grimaced as they approached the study. "Yes, Miss Moir. He is."

"You were expecting to join us then, Lady Rebecca?" The Duke smiled, his voice booming across the room towards her, but there was a steadiness in his gaze that spoke of a serious nature. Rebecca nodded but said nothing, turning towards Lord Hastings as he came towards both she and Miss Moir.

"This is a very serious matter."

The Duke continued on as Rebecca took Lord Hastings' hand for a moment, allowing him to lead her towards a chair. "Lord Hastings has told me a little bit of his brother's darker endeavors of late, but it is the current predicament which I find to be most extraordinary. You say Lord Richards is present in my house without my awareness of it?"

Rebecca glanced at Lord Hastings, but he did not look at her.

"Yes, Your Grace," he replied. "You must forgive me for my forwardness in that. I thought it best. To be truthful, I did not know exactly what to do. My concern was for Lord Richard's safety and the fact that he begged me to keep news of his arrival from you convinced me. After all he had endured thus far, I felt myself obliged to do as he asked. He doubted everyone, including myself."

"Which I can quite understand," Rebecca added, looking back towards the Duke. "He endured a great deal and was injured in the most dreadful way. It would not be fair to expect such a thing from him."

"He believes you now, however?"

Lord Hastings nodded. "Yes. I believe he does."

Rebecca smiled quietly, just as the study door opened and Lord Richards stepped in. Her eyes went back to the Duke, seeing how his eyes flared in obvious surprise. Perhaps he had not believed there was a gentleman staying in one of the servants' bedchambers but now, of course, he could not doubt it.

"Your Grace." Lord Richards bowed.

"Well, I am glad to say you made it to my house party after all," the Duke remarked, levity filling his words. "But if all Lord Hastings has told me is true, then I am greatly troubled to hear it." Gesturing to a chair, he thereafter folded his arms across his chest. "Tell me precisely what happened."

Lord Richards went to sit in a chair to the right of the door, whilst Lord Hastings came to stand behind Rebecca's chair. The Duke of Meyrick simply stood at his desk, overseer over them all.

Taking in an audible breath, Lord Richards set his elbows on his knees and leaned forward in his chair. "As I have told Lord Hastings, I met his brother when we were playing cards together at some occasion or other – I do not remember specifically. To be truthful, I lost the game and garnered a debt, which I paid the following day. You can imagine my surprise when I received a letter from Mr. Shelbourne stating I had not paid what he had asked. In great confusion, I replied to his letter, stating perhaps he had forgotten." Passing one hand over his eyes, he shrugged both shoulders. "In hindsight, that was my mistake. I ought not to have even acknowledged the letter, knowing full well my debt was paid. However, I did so and shortly thereafter, received another letter. This time, it stated the amount had increased due to my lack of payment. I wanted very much to inform him he was wrong so I went to meet with him."

Rebecca's stomach lurched, seeing how Lord Richards closed his eyes. Obviously, the meeting had not gone well.

"My brother did not behave well, I assume." Lord Richards nodded in answer to Lord Hastings' question.

"He did not," he agreed. "There was an attack –it was not particularly grievous, but it was made clear to me that more of the same would occur, if I did not do as was asked. Initially, I was determined to pay the debt, but thereafter, in the days when I recovered, I told myself I would not be cheated out of my wealth."

"And thus, you gave him nothing more?"

Lord Richards nodded. "I did not. I do not know how Mr. Shelbourne knew I was to be attending the Duke's house party but regardless, he found me here and accosted me as I attempted to make my way to the house."

The Duke turned his attention towards Rebecca and the writhing of nerves in Rebecca's stomach increased all the more. "And this is what you witnessed, Lady Rebecca?"

Swallowing, she took in a breath. "I did." Briefly, she told to the Duke of Meyrick what she had seen, ending with the fact that Mr. Shelbourne had attempted to ride over Lord Richards, shuddering as she did so.

"Lady Rebecca is the reason I was not as badly injured as I could have been," Lord Richard acknowledged. "I was not left to lie on the cold ground for any length of time. She sent for Lord Hasting and, thus, I was brought into your house. Forgive me for being unwilling to have my presence made known to you at the time. The truth is, I was afraid. I did not know where Mr. Shelbourne could be. I was frightened that he was somewhere in the house and could easily come to attack me again, should he know of my presence here."

The Duke shook his head. "There is no need for apology. I quite understand it. This is horrific to hear and I am sorry such a thing took place on my property. Mr. Shelbourne is not a gentleman, not in any way. I am sorry to say it, Lord Hastings, but your brother is nothing more than a scoundrel of the worst sort."

Rebecca reached up to press her hand over Lord Hastings as it rested on her shoulder, sure those words would have pained him.

"I am all too aware of that, Your Grace," he replied quietly. "I have spent years attempting to curb his behavior, attempting to bring about change so that our family name could be protected, but my efforts have all been in vain. Perhaps now is the time for his sins to be exposed, for I am believing it is the only way to prevent him from living in such a way any longer."

The Duke harrumphed, looking around the room at them all, one after the other. Miss Moir was the only one who had not said a thing, but she sat at the back of the room, her eyes wide but still, she said nothing. Rebecca offered her a small smile and her friend managed a nod, confirming that, yes, she had paid attention to everything being said but was quite overcome by it all.

"I will have someone fetch Mr. Shelbourne here at once." The Duke rang the bell, but nothing happened. No one came in and it took Rebecca a moment to realize the Duke had prepared the staff already. No doubt, when he did such a thing, Mr. Shelbourne was to be brought to him without delay.

"I have no doubt that Shelbourne will attempt to say he has done none of this. But that is why you are so important, Lady Rebecca, for you are a witness. You saw everything and thus Lord Richards can be protected."

Rebecca nodded but said nothing to Lord Hastings' words. Rather, she looked up at him, seeing the flickering smile dance across his lips before it faded to nothing. Everything hung on Mr. Shelbourne's arrival and what he would say when he was presented with the truth. What would he do when his sins were laid bare? She could only pray that the man would listen, would accept, and would be willing to change his ways, although she did not believe such a thing was possible, given all that Lord Hastings had told her about his brother. She prayed that the next few minutes would remain quiet and calm, with Mr. Shelbourne himself not giving into anger.

And then, she told herself, once this matter was at an end, she would finally have her conversation with Lord Hastings. She would find out everything about their ending of their closeness, would beg him to tell her the truth. Otherwise, she could see no way forward and that, she was sure, would lead to utter darkness for them both.

CHAPTER THIRTEEN

*I*t was difficult to hide his nerves when his brother walked into the room. For so long, Myles had been dealing with the situation entirely alone, struggling to work through all the difficulties his brother brought with him, trying to find ways to make certain that how his brother chose to behave did not reflect poorly on the family name and, therefore, doing his best to keep his own reputation as pristine as possible.

Now, however, he was giving up.

It was proving impossible to stop his brother, for Shelbourne's hand continually turned towards evil. Myles did not know how many gentlemen he had cheated and how many had been threatened, but he was sure there were a good many. In removing Shelbourne's financial security, no doubt Myles had caused injuries to others, for his brother would have gained a great deal of coin in some other way.

And thus it was now time for others to know of it. He could not simply stand by and allow Shelbourne to continue, not when his brother was now pursuing physical harm towards those he deemed guilty of keeping things from him. Not that Myles believed in any way that Lord Richards – or anyone else for that matter, would owe his brother anything. It had all been some scheme, some wickedness he had dragged others into. If his good name was to be dragged down, then Myles acknowledged he would simply have to accept the consequences of it. There could be no other way. He knew that now.

"Perhaps once Mr. Shelbourne has come in, Miss Moir, you might shut the door behind him? There is a key in the lock. Please, turn it and thereafter hand it to Lord Hastings. We will have to make certain that Shelbourne cannot escape."

Miss Moir nodded, although she looked rather terrified to Myles' eyes. There was nothing said thereafter, with a quiet tension flooding the room, making his heart quicken. Quite what the Duke planned to do, Myles did not know, but he was sure it would be made very clear such behavior could no longer continue. Whatever was to happen, Myles was ready to accept it all, even if it meant being pushed further from Lady Rebecca than he had ever been before.

That thought sent a stab of pain through his heart, but he sucked in air and lifted his chin. He wanted the very best for Lady Rebecca, and if that meant she was to find herself in the arms of another, then he would not begrudge it. Her father's eagerness to care for his daughter was heartfelt – and to place her beside a gentleman who was shamed and spurned by all of society would not be wise. He understood that although Myles was ready to admit that Lady Rebecca would always be in his heart no matter what happened, no matter how far apart they were.

The door was suddenly pushed open and Myles' heart now began throwing itself against his chest. Shelbourne sauntered in, a broad smile on his face, only to come to a complete stop, his grin shattering in a single second. Miss Moir slammed the door hard, turning the key before Shelbourne could react, although the sound itself was jarring, causing Shelbourne to turn sharply.

Myles moved forward quickly, ready to take the key from Miss Moir, wanting to make certain she was protected. "I thank you." Taking it from her, he placed it into his pocket, returning to stand behind Lady Rebecca, fully aware that as yet his brother had not said a single word.

"Come in, Shelbourne." The Duke gestured to a chair, but Shelbourne tipped his head, his hands going behind his back as he stood stock still.

His eyes turned towards Myles. "And what lies has my brother been telling you, Your Grace?"

"There are no lies spoken here this afternoon."

At the sound of Lord Richards' voice, Myles saw his brother start in surprise and then twist his head in the direction of where Lord Richards was sitting. Because he was so far to Shelbourne's left, and because his brother had been so determined to stare at Myles, he clearly had been unaware of Lord Richards' presence. Immediately, Shelbourne shifted from foot to foot as though he intended to pace up and down the room but was unable to do so.

"Lord Richards, I... I did not expect to see you."

"I confess I am concerned to hear what has been said about you," the Duke murmured quietly. "Lord Richards has been residing in my home without my knowledge, mostly because of his fear as to what you might do to him should his presence here be discovered. You injured him severely, and rather than going to make certain he was not badly injured, you not only rode over him but left him on the ground, where he might easily have succumbed to the cold!"

Immediately – and just as Myles had expected – his brother shook his head furiously, feverishly protesting his innocence. "I do not know who has said such a thing, Your Grace, but I can assure you I did no such thing."

Rather than immediately state to Shelbourne that there had been a witness, the Duke merely lifted one eyebrow. Lady Rebecca caught her breath, but Myles gently pressed her shoulder, silently asking her to stay quiet for the time being. She glanced up at him, but to his relief, said nothing.

"You say you did none of the things that Lord Richards has accused you of. You did not gesticulate so furiously that he toppled. You did not look at him lying there injured and instead of helping him, you did *not* ride your horse over him. You did not leave him behind in the chill and the cold."

Shelbourne threw up his hands. "Of course I did not. I could never do such a thing as that! Lord Richards must be speaking of someone else. Mayhap he became confused after his fall. Either that or he is a lying about me for some reason of his own."

"And why would he do such a thing as that?" the Duke asked immediately, sending a sharp look towards Lord Richard, who began to protest. "From what I can see, there can be no reason for the gentleman to do such a thing. Are you well acquainted?"

Shelbourne lifted his chin. "We are acquainted. Lord Richards owes me a significant amount of coin. He states he has paid the debt, but he has not."

"That is a lie." Immediately Lord Richards practically threw himself from his chair, his face blazing with anger, his shoulders hunched and one finger pointed out towards Shelbourne. "You say nothing but lies."

Shelbourne had tipped his head towards Lord Richards,

a slight narrowing of his gaze as he did so. "You may have attempted to threaten me into repaying a debt I have paid once already and believe me, the fear of it has almost persuaded me to do as you asked, only for your brother to make me all too aware that you might easily take advantage of me again if I were to do such a thing." His voice was tight, his face red, eyes flashing and his frame a little bent, such was his anger. "I am a gentleman. I am a gentleman of *honor*, and I have paid your debt, just as you know I have. You seek to gain more from me and think to threaten me into submission. But you have one flaw in that plan."

A wry laugh broke from Shelbourne's lips. "This is all nonsense," he said, throwing out one hand towards the Duke as though he ought to garner the man's sympathy in some way. "I do not know what Lord Richards is speaking of. If you wish to pay me the money you owe, then I would be very glad of it, but I have not been hounding you."

Unable to prevent himself from speaking, Myles cleared his throat. "You need not pretend you are a gentleman of honor, brother. The Duke of Meyrick, Lord Richards, Lady Rebecca and Miss Moir are all too aware of your many, many flaws, and the fact that you are attempting to keep them secret is, quite frankly, ridiculous. I have told them everything. I have told them of the times I have had to try and pull you away from the evil you have surrounded yourself with, of the many times I have ended a scheme of yours and even paid recompense to those you have injured. I have taken away your fortune, I have taken away almost everything I could from you and yet you are determined to make as much of a mess of our family name as you are of your own life. For many years, I have been attempting to protect not only myself, but our family's name and reputation. I have lost a good deal because of it." A knot came into his throat, but he swallowed it away, also aware that the most precious thing he had lost was none other than the woman who sat in front of him. "This has to end, Shelbourne. The Duke knows of your character. He knows of your darkness and he knows Lord Richards is speaking the truth"

At this, his brother merely snorted, rolling his eyes as though Myles had said something truly foolish. "Again, you speak nonsense, brother." Shaking his head in a somewhat pitying fashion, he took in a long breath and then let it out with such a slowness that Myles grasped his fingers into a fist so he would not lose his temper. His brother was attempting to make a fool of him, but he had spent far too long being taken for a fool. This was not to be one of those times.

"As I said," Lord Richards continued. "There is a flaw in your plan. There is a reason the Duke knows I am speaking the truth and that is because everything you did was witnessed by none other than Lady Rebecca,"

Myles felt Lady Rebecca's shoulders lift a little as Shelbourne turned his eyes towards her. The confident smile that had been on his lips now cracked and broke as he looked into her face, no doubt realizing now his intentions of remaining innocent by way of his own lies were slowly falling apart. Nothing was said. Silence flooded the entirety of the room, and it was all Myles could do not to say a single word.

"You have not been able to escape your evil deeds this time," the Duke interrupted quietly, breaking the silence between them all. "Lady Rebecca did not even know what it was she saw, but she saw everything you did. It was she who went to Lord Richards' aid, she who called Lord Hastings, and in doing so, she has found you guilty. Nothing that you can say or do can shake this from your shoulders. You have been discovered, your threats towards Lord Richards have been found out and your guilt has been made clear to us all."

After some moments, Shelbourne shook his head. Myles frowned, wondering at his brother's reaction, although he did not have to wait for long for an explanation.

"What is it you are doing, brother?" Shelbourne turned towards both Myles and Lady Rebecca, coming towards him slowly. "Are you truly going to allow this young woman to tell fabricated lies about me? Do you know how much this will injure us? All those years of attempting to protect our family name, and you will now throw it away simply because of the word of this young lady, a lady who you do not know?"

Myles made to say something, but Lady Rebecca spoke before he could do so. With a lift of her chin, she sat a little forward in her chair. "It should be a great shame for you to know your brother trusts the word of someone he does not know particularly well, over the word of his brother." Her voice was cool and clear, echoing softly around the room. "I saw everything. I believe every word Lord Richards and Lord Hastings have told me about the situation and your guilt is plain to see. You ought to be ashamed of your actions, but yet all you do is seek to place the blame on someone else's shoulders, rather than accept responsibility. You are not a gentleman." She shook her head, turning her face away as well. She could not even bear to look at him. "You are a coward."

The ice in Shelbourne's stare was enough to cause even Myles to quail, for it was as if he hated Lady Rebecca, as though he despised her for being a witness to his cruelty, as though she were the one at fault. Instinctively, Myles took a small step closer and settled his other hand on her shoulder, wanting her to feel protected, wanting his brother to see there was nothing he could do or say to Lady Rebecca that would not have consequences.

"I believe every word that has been said. There can be no doubt, Mr. Shelbourne." The Duke spoke clearly, taking some of the tension from the moment. "I will make you a promise also – there will be others who will come to know of this and, no doubt, more who tell us what you have done to them." His voice was filled with an authority Myles knew he could never have, for he did not have the same standing and position in society as the Duke – but at this moment, he was not jealous but grateful for it. It looked as though his brother *could* be forced to a course of action he did not want to take.

With the Duke's knowledge of Shelbourne's behavior, there could be no escape, not now, and whatever consequences such knowledge brought with it, Myles greeted them with open arms.

"You cannot simply believe the word of a lady. She does not know exactly what it was she witnessed. She is mistaken! Young ladies often are; their heads are much too full of nonsense to be accurate."

Lady Rebecca let out a broken laugh. "Shelbourne, no. Now it is *you* who is simply speaking nonsense in the hope someone will believe you. Do you not understand? Your words are no longer something anyone will listen to."

"And you, brother," Shelbourne continued, as though he had not heard Lady Rebecca. "How could you betray me?" Rounding on him, as though Myles was the one who had somehow done such a great wrong, he glared at him. "What about brotherly loyalty?"

"Loyalty is not a word you understand." Myles lifted his chin as the Duke nodded slowly, clear in his agreement with

Myles' statement. "I have tried my best, and you have thrown every attempt back at me. My requests have fallen on deaf ears. My begging you to consider our family honor has been repeatedly ignored. I trust every word Lady Rebecca has told me of what she saw of your interaction with Lord Richards."

Lifting his shoulders, he sent his brother his sorrowful smile. "The truth is, Shelbourne, you are untrustworthy. You are unscrupulous and you are not worthy of another modicum of my time nor my efforts. I cannot give you anything more, and the truth of your actions must come out, if there is to be any change. Until you accept that, until you see the dark path you have been walking and turn from it, then I must push you far away from me. Should you, in truth, come to me and ask for my aid, then it will be given freely and that is a promise I shall hold to my heart for as long as I am required to."

Shelbourne shook his head but said nothing, his jaw suddenly tight. Lord Richards shifted slightly in his chair, not looking at Shelbourne, but rather turning his attention to Lady Rebecca. She nodded back at him, as though agreeing the situation had now come to a swift conclusion – and Shelbourne saw it.

"You fell off your horse of your own accord!" The explosion from Shelbourne's lips caught everyone in the room. Lady Rebecca started violently, feeling the very same shock that ran through Myles' veins. Having just spent the last few minutes declaring that such a thing had never happened, that he had not met Lord Richards on the grounds and that Lady Rebecca did not know what she had seen, Shelbourne had now declared his guilt for all to see. Myles' heart ached, not with a sense of joy, but rather with overwhelming sadness. It appeared his brother could never be redeemed from such a path. He was a man much too used to lying, too used to concocting wickedness. Except now, his lies had tied him to his guilt.

"You are no longer welcome in my house." The Duke's voice was low, and he spoke quietly as Shelbourne immediately pushed both hands through his hair, letting out a groan, either with awareness over the foolishness of what he had just said, or anger at being treated so. "Society will know of this. I will do my best to make it clear your brother has done all that he can to prevent you from spreading anymore cruelty, but you have rejected him. I am sorry his name will be tarnished but both he and I are aware it must be done to protect the rest of society from your wicked hands."

Setting both hands on his desk, the Duke leaned forward over it, his gaze fixed. "Understand this, Shelbourne. No one will welcome you, not once they have heard from me. You will no longer be welcomed at the gambling table. You will not be asked to any social events. You will be rejected, cut off from those you have sought to exploit for so long. There ought to be nothing but shame in your heart and yet, I believe that at this moment all you feel is anger, rather than disgrace."

"I wish it did not have to be this way, brother." Despite the fact Shelbourne had brought him so much pain and discontent for so long, there was still a part of Myles that longed for reconciliation, for him to regain the brother he had once known, and yet he was quite sure now such a thing could never be. "I shall always be your brother, however. If you are in dire need, circumstances are such that you simply have nowhere else to turn, I will be there – although there shall never again be any monetary offering, you understand."

Silence grew between them until Shelbourne moved closer, his jaw tight, his eyes blazing. "You are rejecting me."

Lady Rebecca rose before Myles could speak. Much to his astonishment, she stepped forward, putting one hand on Shelbourne's arm and looking up at him with a steadiness Myles had never expected from her.

"Your brother is not rejecting you. You have pushed him away. These consequences are yours to bear, if you wish to accept them as such. You will no doubt, wish to blame everyone else. Perhaps, in time, you will have the courage to accept your own guilt. Good day. Mr. Shelbourne."

Myles came forward, glancing at the Duke, who nodded. Walking to his brother, he said nothing, merely holding Shelbourne's gaze for a moment before turning away. Lady Rebecca held out her hand to him and he seized it before walking to the door, setting in the key and then stepping through it.

Leaving his brother behind.

CHAPTER FOURTEEN

"I am so very excited for the ball!" Miss Moir clasped Rebecca's arm, her excited eyes roving around the room. "I am very glad the matter with Lord Hastings' brother has been resolved. Do you feel a good deal more freedom now?"

Rebecca gave her friend a small smile, but only shrugged her shoulders by way of response. There had been a brief discussion in the hallway in the moments thereafter, for Miss Moir and Lord Richards had joined them, but since then, Lord Hastings had been absent. He had not been at dinner that day, nor had he been at the evening entertainment. She had not seen him at breakfast, at luncheon or this afternoon when they had all stepped out for a winter's walk. At dinner, he had yet again been absent from them all and she had not dared to ask the Duke of Meyrick as to where he had gone.

It seemed the other guests had not even noticed Lord Hastings' absence, nor even Miss Moir, given that she had not mentioned it. Praying perhaps he would be here at the Christmas ball, she looked around eagerly, desperately hoping to see him... but his face did not show itself in the crowd. Rebecca's heart was heavy as she closed her eyes briefly. Had the matter with his brother made Lord Hastings absent himself from everything – including her? Was he overcome with misery? Or had something more taken place?

"You are looking for Lord Hastings?" Miss Moir smiled softly. "I do not think he is here as yet."

Rebecca sighed. "No, he is not."

"That is a little strange. I would have thought that he would be eager to be by your side the moment you stepped into the ballroom."

"I do not think he is here at all." Miserably, Rebecca's heart ached with grief and suddenly the noise, the laughter, the smiles and the music were all too much. It fought against the sadness that filled her and she could no longer bear it. "Forgive me. I think... I think I need to excuse myself for a short while."

Before her friend could ask where she was going, Rebecca had turned into the crowd of guests. The Duke was throwing one ball each week, it seemed, but yet her heart could not find a single second of happiness at present. Not certain as to where she was going, Rebecca found herself walking to the front of the house. Most of the guests had already arrived, but the doors were still open and despite the cold, despite the chill that ran towards her, brushing over her skin, Rebecca stepped outside.

Making her way down the stone steps, she lifted her hands to rub up her arms, taking in a deep breath as she made her way to the left of the house. Needing to walk only a short distance and finding the cold winter's air the breath that she needed, tears came into her eyes as she considered what had passed between Lord Hastings and his brother.

There had been great sadness in that moment when Lord Hastings had separated himself from Shelbourne, certainly, but also with it had come a relief – she had seen it in his face as he had walked from the room. Relief that his brother would no longer be this great weight that rested upon his shoulders, that he was no longer alone in his struggles.

But where has he gone now? Dropping her head, she let out a long breath, frosting the air. If Lord Hastings was no longer at the Duke's manor house, then where could he be?

"Lady Rebecca!"

She turned sharply, her heart spiraling as she saw the face of none other than the very gentleman she had been thinking of, lit by the fiery lanterns at the front of the house as well as by the moon itself. He was breathing hard and, to her surprise, she noticed him dressed in warm traveling clothes. There was no hat on his head and his dark hair looked disheveled.

"Lord Hastings?" Hardly able to believe it, she took a moment to catch her breath. "You – you have returned. I thought you were absent, and I feared..."

She caught his fingers. His breath was warm across her cheeks as she looked up into his face. Seeing him smile, her heart cried out for him and it was all she could do not to step forward and embrace him. There was more that she had to understand before such a thing could happen.

"It is a blessing your father's estate does not lie too far from here." After releasing her hand, he took off his coat and flung it around her shoulders. "I did what I should have done the first time we grew close, Lady Rebecca. I went to speak to your father."

Her eyes flared as she caught her breath, staring up at him. "Truly?"

Nodding, Lord Hastings brushed his hand lightly down

her cheek. "We should step inside. There is a lot for me to tell you."

"No." She shook her head. "I am not cold. Speak here, where we might be alone for just a few minutes, I beg of you. What with the ball, my mother will no doubt think I am in the corner with some gentleman exchanging a kiss or two, given she seems to have lost all sense of propriety. She certainly will not be looking for me." This was said with a wry smile, but Lord Hastings immediately caught his breath, although she could not understand why. "I have not shared a Christmas kiss with any gentleman, however. I should not want you to think otherwise."

At this, Lord Hastings chuckled, his shoulders dropping and Rebecca blushed, realizing now why he had caught his breath. "I will not pretend I am not relieved to hear it," he replied. "Let us remain here, close to the house, but we ought not to be out for long. I am afraid you will become very cold indeed."

Agreeing, Rebecca turned to face him a little more and, at once, Lord Hastings began to speak as though there had been so much to tell her that he did not want to waste a single moment.

"The reason I went to speak to your father is because I am aware our connection has grown close again. Whilst I am certain of my desire, I cannot speak for you. However, should there be even the smallest hint you wished to, once more, return to what was the beginning of something quite wonderful, something I am all too aware that I ruined, then I wanted to make certain your father knew of it."

This was all said in a great rush and, a little surprised, Rebecca lifted both eyebrows as she blinked quickly. "Did you ask him if he would grant you permission to court me?"

Lord Hastings shook his head, pressing his lips tight

together as he turned his head away. After a moment, he turned and offered her his arm. She took it at once, her heart floundering suddenly given the serious expression that was now on his face as they ambled slowly back towards the front door of the house.

"Your father realized our connection in the summer Season, Lady Rebecca." His shoulders dropped as he looked at her, his face sorrowful. "Lord Wilbram spoke to me one evening, stating that I was not permitted to be close to you. It turns out he was aware of my brother's wickedness and had, in fact, fallen into several of my brother's schemes. He had not lost a significant amount of money, but it was enough to bring him some embarrassment, and thus he was determined that his daughter – the daughter of an Earl – could never be permitted to have a connection with someone such as myself. The truth was, I had hidden our closeness as best I could as I attempted to resolve things with my brother. I was afraid that if the worst happened and all of society knew of Shelbourne's deceit and trickery, you would be injured by your connection with me. I was afraid for your reputation and standing in society – and I beg you to understand I did so out of care and concern for you, nothing more. Perhaps it was foolish. Perhaps I should have been open and honest with you about my brother, but I was afraid."

Her heart was beating so furiously that Rebecca's breathing was coming quick and fast, even though they were walking at a slow pace. It was as she had feared. Her father *had* been the one to push her and Lord Hastings apart – but, to her mind, for quite the wrong reason. Closing her eyes briefly, she took in a breath and then snuggled a little more closely into him, putting her other hand on his own. "What was it you were afraid of?"

"I was afraid you would reject me. If you knew the depths of depravity that my brother had fallen into, then would you really wish to be associated with someone such as myself? My feelings for you are significant and my heart so filled with longing that I could not bring myself to tell you the truth. In hindsight, that was very wrong. I should have trusted you. I should have told you everything and accepted whatever consequences followed, just as I have done now when it came to my brother. In keeping it hidden, I hid my heart. Your father told me to stay far from you and having no alternative, I promised to do so, for, whilst I felt unfairly treated, I understood his concern."

Cold winter air flooded Rebecca's lungs. It had been as she had suspected then. Her father had been attempting to protect her by setting her far from Lord Hastings, but had never once told her himself. She did not think it fair that such a gentleman should be treated so when his brother was the one that had done wrong.

"When I put that note on your bed. I had no intention of telling you about your father's part in all of this. I only intended to tell you all about my brother and to admit I should have been honest with you about him from the beginning. I have been foolish, I think. I have given so much of my time and my energy into protecting my family's reputation instead of accepting that my brother was intent on ruination. If I had been honest to the entirety of society, then mayhap I could have distanced myself from him and accepted the embarrassment that came with it regardless."

Rebecca closed her eyes. "And yet I can understand why you wished to keep it as secret as you could," she answered him softly. "I think I must seek your forgiveness also, for I have believed you were a gentleman without honor, and yet, now I see that, in ending our closeness so abruptly and without explanation, you were doing what you could to protect my relationship with my father."

Lord Hastings turned, his hands holding hers as they came to a stop. "I was very unhappy with his decision. I was angry and yet I had to admit I understood his concern and his reluctance." The gentleness in his voice made her eyes close. She did not feel cold, but rather, it was as though she were standing next to a blazing furnace, warmth flooding into every part of her. Everything that had been jagged and broken between them smoothed itself out and it filled her with joy to feel it.

"You are an honorable gentleman. More honorable than I have ever thought you. Had I known the truth, then –"

"But you did not know the truth." His hand released hers, but instead lifted her chin slightly so she had no other choice but to look into his face. "As I have said, I have spoken with your father. I have made it plain that my brother will no longer be allowed to behave in the same manner as he has been. I told him everything, in fact. I told him what you had witnessed and how the Duke is involved. I stated this will curb my brother's endeavors to further his wickedness in any way he can."

Rebecca's gaze faltered as his fingers caressed her cheek. "And has he accepted that?"

A gentle laugh followed her question. "He accepted it, certainly, but I believe he intends to write to you. He has said to me that your choice is to be your own, but he will urge you to consider carefully, to think of everything that could occur should you accept me."

Rebecca smiled, thinking of all the wonderful things that could take place should she come close to Lord Hastings again. "I do not think there is much left for me to consider! I am aware of everything now, and I am so very grateful for all you have told me. I have seen your character to be just as I once believed it to be and I am sorry I ever considered otherwise. To know your heart has never turned from me is a wonder in itself."

His hand went to the back of her neck, his hand gently stroking the soft skin there, and Rebecca shivered lightly. "No, Lady Rebecca. My heart has never turned from you. It has cried, and it has wept over our separation, but I... I have never forgotten you. My heart has belonged to you since the first moment we met, I believe. There have been moments I have wished for, moments when my longing can be fulfilled and I –"

Seeing his head lower, Rebecca caught her breath and closed her eyes – only for her name to be called by someone.

"Lady Rebecca!"

She turned quickly, more than a little irritated at having been interrupted by what was going to be, she was sure, one of the most wonderful moments of her life. To her surprise, Miss Moir hurried forward, her face a little flushed.

"Lady Rebecca. Lord Hastings." Miss Moir pressed both hands to her cheeks, clearly embarrassed at what she had stepped into. "Forgive me for the interruption, but your mother has been eagerly searching for you these last few minutes. I have told her you had a requirement to go to the powder room, but that will not keep her satisfied for long, particularly if you are away for a longer duration than she expects."

Closing her eyes, Rebecca huffed out a breath, trying to hold back her billowing frustration. "It seems as though we shall have to continue this conversation another time, as has so often been the case these last few weeks." With a smile, she pressed his hand. "I am so very glad to see you return. I hope that much is clear, at least!"

Lord Hastings chuckled. "You have certainly made that *very* clear, and I assure you the sentiment is returned. I will attend the ball in a short while. I should return to my room and change, for I do not wish to turn up to the ball with my travelling clothes still upon me. I think to do so would raise a good many eyebrows!"

Despite her frustration, Rebecca laughed and shrugged out of his coat. "Indeed. I will be waiting for your arrival, Lord Hastings. In fact, I shall be looking for it."

"Perhaps you might save me the waltz?" he asked her. "It is to be the supper dance at the end of the evening I believe."

She nodded. "Yes, that is so, and I would be very glad indeed to keep it for you, my Lord."

Miss Moir tugged at her arm gently. Rebecca was forced to step away. A small but contented sigh left her lips as she made her way back indoors, hardly feeling the cold winter air wrap around her shoulders. Assuming she would be in Lord Hastings' arms again, dancing with him, knowing there was nothing to keep them apart from each other. She understood everything now, and felt a great relief come to her. Every muscle in her body allowed her to breathe deeply as a bright smile spread across her face.

"I think this is the happiest I have ever seen you!" Miss Moir exclaimed, as they made their way back to the ball once more. "I assume you are very glad to see Lord Hastings return to the Duke's house."

"I certainly am," Rebecca replied, letting out a small, happy sigh as she stepped into the ballroom. "And, in fact, I look forward to dancing with him all the more. This evening shall be the most wonderful one of the entire house party, and I cannot tell you how eager I am to return to it."

CHAPTER FIFTEEN

Returning to Lord Wilbram's estate had been an action of instinct. The idea had come to him in a single moment and Myles had acted upon it straight away. He had not stopped for a single moment, had not had time nor opportunity – nor even desire – to tell Lady Rebecca where it was he was going. There had been a concern he would leave her with lingering anxiety with regard to whether or not her father would speak with him favorably.

As his valet finished dressing Myles for the evening, Myles gazed into the looking glass, noting the expression on his face at present was not one that had often been on his face these last few months. There was a softness about his features that had not been there for some time, the heavy grooves on his forehead now faded, his brown eyes no longer as dark as he had often seen them. There was even a smile across his lips that sent a light into them all the more – and in his heart, Myles knew such a change had been brought about all because of Lady Rebecca.

Had she not asked for his aid on that winter's afternoon, then he would never have been given this opportunity to find a way back to her. In a way, his brother's misdeeds had brought both he and Lady Rebecca back towards each other, although he could not be glad for his brother's evil works nor the injuries he had brought to Lord Richards.

His eyes were drawn to his dressing table and to the silver bracelet that belonged to Lady Rebecca, the one she had given to him after the Christmas parlor game. As yet he had not returned it to her, but now he felt the moment was right.

When the valet stepped back, his preparations finished, Myles gave himself one final look in the mirror and, with a nod, turned from the room. His heart was already filling with excitement over the Christmas ball, glad to know that not only would Lady Rebecca be looking for him, but that there would also be a waltz where he might again hold her close. There was nothing between them any longer – no secrets, no shame, no pain of separation. It was a situation he had never found himself in before and the sense of freedom made his steps quicken all the more.

The noise in the ballroom was overwhelming and it took Myles a few moments to adjust himself to it. The house party appeared to become all the more raucous every time there was a ball – and there appeared to be one every week at present – but Myles was glad for the additional crush of people. It meant he would be able to move close to Lady Rebecca without garnering any overt attention, for his intention at present was to pull her away from the rest of the guests if he could, in order to restore the silver bracelet to her.... and, if she would permit him, steal his Christmas kiss.

"Lord Hastings."

Turning, his smile spread wide across his face at the sight of Lady Rebecca. Her cheeks were flushed, but her smile blossomed across her delicate features. "I did tell you I would be looking for your arrival, did I not?"

"Indeed, you did," he laughed, only for his eyes to rove across the crowded ballroom. "Your mother was not overly concerned, then?"

Lady Rebecca shook her head, her hazel eyes dancing. "My dear mother was eager for me to meet a particular gentleman, that is all." Her eyes softened gently as she smiled at him. "But I do not feel the need to do such a thing."

Wishing desperately that he might pull her into his arms at this very moment, Myles satisfied himself with a brief touch of his hand on hers. "The waltz will be starting soon," he murmured. "I am eager for it to begin so we might be close to each other again."

As if the orchestra had heard him speak, at that very moment, the next music for the waltz began, playing for only a few moments before fading away again, leaving time for the gentlemen to go in search of the ladies they were to dance with before they stepped out onto the floor. With a broad smile and hope in his heart, Myles offered his arm to Lady Rebecca and together they walked out onto the floor.

"There is a mistletoe bough, Lord Hastings. We shall dance by it." Lady Rebecca smiled at him, lifting her eyebrows gently. "If we just stop underneath it, you must take pause to take one of the berries for ourselves."

"Pity the poor gentleman who finds himself underneath the bough without a single berry left," he laughed quietly. "What a great disappointment that would be. If there are no berries left, then no kisses can be taken."

"Then let us pray we are not the ones so unfortunate." The look in Lady Rebecca's eyes sent billowing flame burning up through his core and suddenly, Myles was desperate to make *certain* they stopped underneath the mistletoe. In fact, he eyed it eagerly, wondering just how quickly he could move both himself and Lady Rebecca towards it.

He was to be given only a few moments, however, for the music began again and with a bow and with great joy in his heart, Myles stepped forward, clasping one hand lightly around Lady Rebecca's waist whilst his other hand held tight to hers. Their steps together flowed flawlessly, moving as one even though his attention was fully on the lady in his arms rather than on the music. Her gaze was on his, holding steady as the dance continued and he could look nowhere else save for her face, delighting himself in what he saw there.

Ever since the summer Season, he had found himself growing increasingly drawn to Lady Rebecca. There had been interest, then affection, and thereafter, something more that Myles had not fully understood – and when they had been forced to separate, his heart had been broken into fragmented pieces, the bits of which he was still collecting even at this very moment. The desperation to reconcile himself to her had lingered in his heart for many months, growing steadily until he had been desperate for an opportunity to do so. In seeing her here, it had been as though fate were giving him another chance but it had not been until earlier that evening that he had finally been able to tell her everything. How much she must have endured, Myles realized. How much pain and suffering she had dealt with and yet, despite that, still she seemed to be pulled towards him in the same way he felt tied to her. It was more than he could have ever hoped for and even though he was quite certain that Lord Wilbram would never give him his full blessing, that did not seem to matter any longer. If he could make Lady Rebecca happy for the remainder of his days, then that would be enough.

"I am sorry, Lady Rebecca."

She looked up at him, her eyes widening a little as Myles merely smiled.

"I am sorry for the fact I broke off our connection without giving you an explanation of any sort. Yes, I would not have told you about your father but I could have explained to you about my brother. That would have been a reason enough. How much you must have had to deal with in regards to your pain, how much of a struggle and confusion because of me. I am sorry for all of it. Had I been more honest, then I might now find us both in a much happier situation."

"But mayhap such a happy situation can be discovered nonetheless," Lady Rebecca replied as he twirled her around. "Just because one has made a mistake does not mean one cannot resolve it. You have spoken to my father and whilst he may have been a little less willing than we would have expected, he will not hold us back. Your brother brings difficulties and yes, society may step back from you a little but will that matter if I am by your side? If I am on your arm?"

He smiled at her, glanced over her shoulder, and then came to a small, slow stop a little away from the other dancers. "Indeed it would not be, Lady Rebecca. You are quite right. If I have you by my side, then what need have I for anyone else?" Lifting his chin, he tipped his head back to look above him, and then looked over at Lady Rebecca, seeing her do the same. She laughed and then stepped back from him a little as he reached up to pluck one mistletoe berry from the bough.

"We are fortunate, Lady Rebecca, for there are only

three left." Myles' stomach rolled with sudden anticipation, only to look to his left and then to his right, noticing how the other guests watched them. Ladies were laughing, tilting their heads closer to each other and whispering to one another. Glancing around the room as the music continued, Myles bent forward, brushed his lips across Lady Rebecca's cheek, close to the edge of her mouth, and then tugged her gently into his arms again.

The urge to kiss her long and hard did not leave him. The touch of his lips to her cheek shot incredible sensations through him like a roaring fire, sending fierce heat into every part of him. Every inch of his frame was tingling with expectation and anticipation and suddenly, he could not wait for the waltz to finish. He did not *want* to linger any longer. Rather than continue the dance, he slowed their steps again and after a moment stepped away, still grasping Lady Rebecca's hand. When he led her to the side of the ballroom, she went without a question, giggling as he glanced back at her, walking through the crowd. A few heads were turned in their direction, but Myles did not care. All he had to do was find a quiet space where he might tell Lady Rebecca what was burning in his heart.

A door presented itself and, without hesitation, Myles stepped through it. The hallway was quiet, giving them enough of an opportunity to speak quietly given that there were many small, shadowed alcoves and he stepped into one quickly.

Lady Rebecca's breath was coming a little more quickly and Myles winced in embarrassment. Clearly he had been very eager to take her away from the rest of those in the ballroom – perhaps a little too eager.

"Forgive me, Rebecca. I could not wait another moment."

Laughing softly, she shook her head lightly, her hands clasped lightly in front of her. "I am glad you did such a thing – I am of the same mind."

A little relieved, Myles gave her a small smile, before glancing down at his pocket. "I have something of yours." Taking the silver bracelet out of his pocket, he handed it to her, his heart quickening a little. Lady Rebecca took it at once, although her face flushed as she looked up to see his steady gaze.

"You have kept my bracelet for all this time?"

"Yes, I have. Initially, I did so because I wanted to offer it back to you without anything being required for there was a time when I was quite certain that the last thing you wanted from me was such a thing. After my note, and even after our discussions, I was sure all I desired could not be at *all* what you hoped for. I thought to return your silver bracelet to you in a quiet moment, but perhaps now that things have changed between us, now that we are as close as we have ever been, I shall take my forfeit after all."

"I see." Her voice soft, Lady Rebecca pressed both hands to her cheeks for a moment as she looked up at him, her eyes fastening themselves to his. Myles moved a little closer, glad that the shadows hid them from those who wandered in and out of the ballroom. So long as they were quiet, they would not be seen. "I do not think I need to ask what you wish your forfeit to be?"

"A Christmas kiss has long been my wish," he murmured, swallowing hard. "But I will say that such a thing is only requested if you should wish to give it, Lady Rebecca. Otherwise, I will return your bracelet to you without requirement."

Before he could form any further words, Lady Rebecca laughed, flung her arms around his neck, and standing on tiptoes, pressed her mouth to his. Her lips were soft and warm, and such was the intensity of the moment, that Myles took a second to respond before wrapping his arms about her waist, hauling her all the closer to him as he angled his head to deepen their kiss. In that moment, Myles felt every single fragment of his heart sealing itself back into place.

"You must know that my heart is full of love for you, Lady Rebecca." Myles found himself whispering to her, his lips a hair's breadth from hers. "This Christmas has been one of a great many revelations – some darkness, certainly, but at the very end of it all, a great and wonderful light filled with joy. It is a joy that only you have brought me."

Lady Rebecca's hand ran down one side of his face, her fingers pressing lightly against his cheek as she gazed up into his eyes. "I think the reason I could not forget you, I could not push you away was because I was in love with you. I did not expect this Christmas would be one where we would reconcile but I am glad, so very glad, for it. I do not think I have ever been as happy as I am in this moment for there is nothing between us now. There is no need for us to stand apart from each other. Our hearts are one and I would beg of you, Lord Hastings, let us look to our future from this day onwards with one mind. If our hearts are bound, then so must our future be."

"That is my feeling exactly." Myles lifted her hands, kissing first one and then the other, one cheek and then the second before pressing a final kiss to her soft lips. Sighing contentedly, she closed her eyes for a moment longer as Myles looked down at her, thinking just how wondrous a lady she was, how much she had forgiven him for, and how much he adored her. He had no doubt what his future held, for with Lady Rebecca now by his side once more, what else could there be for him but to think of marriage? Yes, there would have to be a courtship but come the summer Season, Myles silently determined in his heart that they should wed. It was all he wanted, all he desired and all his heart yearned for.

"You have been given your Christmas kiss, Lord Hastings." Lady Rebecca's eyes opened and she smiled at him, coming closer to him again so that his hands went about her waist.

"Yes, I have – and with it has come the fulfillment of everything I could have ever hoped for. I love you, Rebecca."

"And I love you, my dear Lord Hastings."

A HAPPY CHRISTMAS for Rebecca and Myles! Check out a story with another happy ending in A Family for Christmas

There is a sneak peek just ahead!

MY DEAR READER

Thank you for reading and supporting my books! I hope this story brought you some escape from the real world into the always captivating Regency world. A good story, especially one with a happy ending, just brightens your day and makes you feel good! If you enjoyed the book, would you leave a review on Amazon? Reviews are always appreciated.

Below is a complete list of all my books! Why not click and see if one of them can keep you entertained for a few hours?

The Duke's Daughters Series
The Duke's Daughters: A Sweet Regency Romance Boxset
A Rogue for a Lady
My Restless Earl
Rescued by an Earl
In the Arms of an Earl
The Reluctant Marquess (Prequel)

A Smithfield Market Regency Romance
The Smithfield Market Romances: A Sweet Regency Romance Boxset
The Rogue's Flower
Saved by the Scoundrel
Mending the Duke
The Baron's Malady

The Returned Lords of Grosvenor Square
The Returned Lords of Grosvenor Square: A Regency Romance Boxset
The Waiting Bride
The Long Return
The Duke's Saving Grace
A New Home for the Duke

The Spinsters Guild
The Spinsters Guild: A Sweet Regency Romance Boxset
A New Beginning
The Disgraced Bride
A Gentleman's Revenge
A Foolish Wager
A Lord Undone

Convenient Arrangements
Convenient Arrangements: A Regency Romance Collection
A Broken Betrothal
In Search of Love
Wed in Disgrace
Betrayal and Lies
A Past to Forget
Engaged to a Friend

Landon House
Landon House: A Regency Romance Boxset
Mistaken for a Rake
A Selfish Heart
A Love Unbroken
A Christmas Match
A Most Suitable Bride

An Expectation of Love

Second Chance Regency Romance
Second Chance Regency Romance Boxset
Loving the Scarred Soldier
Second Chance for Love
A Family of her Own
A Spinster No More

Soldiers and Sweethearts
Soldiers and Sweethearts: A Sweet Regency Romance Boxset
To Trust a Viscount
Whispers of the Heart
Dare to Love a Marquess
Healing the Earl
A Lady's Brave Heart

Ladies on their Own: Governesses and Companions
More Than a Companion
The Hidden Governess
The Companion and the Earl
More than a Governess
Protected by the Companion
A Wager with a Viscount

Lost Fortunes, Found Love
A Viscount's Stolen Fortune

Christmas Stories

Christmas Kisses (Series)
The Lady's Christmas Kiss

Love and Christmas Wishes: Three Regency Romance Novellas
<u>A Family for Christmas</u>
Mistletoe Magic: A Regency Romance
Heart, Homes & Holidays: A Sweet Romance Anthology

Happy Reading!

All my love,

Rose

A SNEAK PEEK OF A FAMILY FOR CHRISTMAS

CHAPTER ONE

It seemed strange, on such a somber occasion as a funeral, that there were boughs of holly, hundreds of candles and garlands of evergreens decorating the church ready for the service to commemorate the beginning of Advent that was due to take place the next day. Anna Campbell looked at the coffin set upon trestles at the altar. It contained the mortal remains of her father, Colin Campbell. The casket was the best she could afford—and had been the cheapest the carpenter could offer. Anna ran a hand over the rough, unvarnished wood and wondered if she would miss him at all.

The vicar's words echoed around the empty church as he performed the final blessing and said a solemn prayer commending Pa to God's mercy. He gave Anna a rueful smile, then nodded to the men hovering at the very back of the church to come and fetch the coffin to take it to the gravesite. They were clad in dark clothes, their boots and breeches covered with mud. They had swarthy complexions from working outside in all weathers. Their expressions were solemn and inscrutable. She could only assume that they were the gravediggers and that the vicar had paid them a few coppers more to come and carry Pa to the gravesite as she had nobody who might do it for her. She nodded to them politely, and they gave her a respectful half-bow, then another to the casket, before they picked it up and began to walk steadily down the aisle.

Anna followed them, the vicar walking just ahead of them all as they carried her father's body towards the doors of the church. The pews were all empty. There was not a soul present to witness Pa's passing or to offer Anna their love and support. It did not surprise Anna that not even one of the more dedicated members of the congregation had come, as they often would for even a stranger that was to be buried. Pa had made too many enemies in his life for anyone to mourn him, much less offer him respect, and she hadn't known if there was anyone she should have told that he had finally succumbed to the evils his whoring, drinking, and gambling had put upon his body. She doubted that even she would miss him.

There was an aunt somewhere. Anna's mother's sister. There had been no contact between them since long before Anna had been born, so she doubted that even they, her only family now, would have wanted to come and pay their respects. Pa had always grumbled that Mama's high-and-mighty sister had never thought Pa good enough—it had always been clear that there was little love lost between them. All Anna knew of Aunt Hannah was her mother's stories of their childhood and the moments when it was clear just how much she missed her sister after Hannah had upped and left home to marry a man who lived in some grand city somewhere. It might have been London, or Liverpool, York, or even Edinburgh. It had never been spoken of, and Anna had been too young to remember the details—Ma had died when Anna was barely five years old, and all she had been left with was an idea that someday she might seek out her aunt so that she could get away from her miserable life with Pa.

The silent quartet made their way out of the church. The weather was mild but damp, making everything smell just a little earthy. The churchyard was sheltered by trees and filled with extravagant monuments to the much-beloved dead. Anna admired the beauty of some of the carvings and sculptures that adorned the graves of the wealthy, buried as close to the church as they could be. She noted the way the extravagance of the closest graves gave way to simple headstones and unadorned crosses as they moved further away from the hallowed vaults of the imposing village church. But they kept on walking. Anna could not afford even as much as had been provided by these families of more modest means. Pa would be buried in a quiet corner, along with many other men who died penniless in recent weeks, with no grave marker of any kind. He would be forgotten by the world.

With a grimace, she thought about the debts her father had left behind. Some she would be able to forget, as they were many years old and it would be unlikely that she would ever see those of her father's creditors again. Many would simply acknowledge that her father could no longer pay and so would consider the debts null and void. But there were too many that would expect her to make good on them, despite knowing she hadn't a sous to her name. Anna had no idea how she would ever make payment of such vast sums, and she feared that she would be followed wherever she might go by some very unsavory characters.

The gravediggers made their way through the churchyard to a boggy corner that was the furthest from the church that was possible and lowered the coffin into the gaping hole in the ground. Inside the hole, Anna could see a number of other rough coffins and even a couple of bodies wrapped in nothing more than a sheet of rough cloth. It made her sad to think that so many men and women ended their days in such a manner, cheek by jowl with people they had not even known. She wondered briefly if like Pa, they deserved such an ignominious end, or if they had been the unfortunate victims of poverty and sickness. She could only hope that what the bible taught was true, that man's earthly remains mattered little—that it was the soul that God cared about. Even for Pa, she prayed that he had done enough good in his life, somewhere, and had repented of his many sins so he might be permitted to enter heaven's gates.

The vicar sprinkled holy water over the grave, said a brief prayer of committal, and it was over. The gravediggers began to shovel the earth piled up beside the grave back into the hole, and the vicar made his way back inside the church —once Anna had handed him a small purse with all the coin she had left in the world. She'd had to sell Pa's wagon and everything in it just to give him this meager funeral. Even men of God needed to be paid their share.

Anna stood at the graveside and watched until the last shovelful of earth was back where it had come from and the gravediggers had moved away. "You got what you deserved," she said bitterly, remembering the beatings she'd gotten over the years. Pa had always been handy with his fists when in his cups, and he had been a sore loser. Anna had always been to blame for everything that had gone wrong in Pa's life, from saddling him with her very presence, to the times when a horse trade fell through because she'd fallen off the half-wild mounts he insisted on selling before they were ready. "But you were all I had, and so I am glad I have done right by you. Rest easy in your grave, Pa."

She walked away, her head held high. Anna had learned early that she needed to hide her feelings and to pretend to be that which she was not. Pa made her play so many roles as part of his many schemes and she'd learned young how to mimic those around her. Now, perhaps those skills would help her to move on and to find a better life. Anna knew that she could speak more eloquently than most of her kind, and she moved with grace. She was sure that she would be able to find a position in a fine house somewhere – even if she had to start at the bottom as a scullery maid or kitchen hand. Anna knew how to work hard – even if Pa never had.

She made her way back to the grand porch of the church and picked up the old carpetbag she had left there. Inside its battered, capacious exterior was everything Anna possessed. A tattered gown and clean undergarments, an old necklace Pa swore had belonged to her mother and a book of poetry she'd found in amongst her mother's old things some years earlier. Anna could barely read them, though she tried hard to do so. She could vaguely remember her mother reading them to her, but the recollection was so hazy and vague Anna often wondered if she'd simply imagined it.

Anna felt that she had known no other life than the one she had shared with Pa, though she knew that things had been very different whilst her mother had been alive. In her memories, Ma was always so much more refined than Pa, she had interests and skills that he had grown to be envious of, sparking his temper and spite. Anna often wondered how differently her life might have been had Ma lived longer. Perhaps she'd be able to read and write, have taken up a place in service and be respectable.

Instead, a life of trading in half-wild horses, card-sharping, and moving from town to town before anyone could catch Pa and demand he repay them had not given Anna many usable skills, other than the ability to act to deceive. She did not wish to continue in the vein that he had followed. His passing was her chance to make a new life, one where she could do good rather than harm. Yet there were few employers that would take on an unskilled, uneducated, and penniless woman such as herself. She'd probably end up having to throw herself on the mercy of the parish, though she vowed to do all she could to avoid such an outcome.

With a last glance at the church, bedecked with greenery for the Christmas celebrations, Anna turned and made her way out onto the street. As she passed through the lychgate, she vowed never to look back. There must be a way that she could turn her life around. There had to be someone or somewhere that she could go where she would not only be welcomed, but she would be useful and could make enough money to support herself. But it would not be here, not in this miserable little village where the chain that bound her had finally been buried.

Feeling more than a little trepidatious, Anna turned left out of the gate, putting Sparsholt behind her, and began to walk along the rutted road that would lead her first to Winchester and then onwards towards Farnham and Guildford. She prayed that there would be some work for her in one of these places, but if there were not, then she would continue onwards towards London. It was the wrong time of year to be searching for work; employers were often too caught up with arranging their Christmas celebrations for family and friends to be doing much business, but she had no choice.

A glimmer of blue began to appear between the clouds in the sky above as she walked briskly along the road to Winchester. Anna couldn't help but feel optimistic as the day progressed and the sun finally appeared, bathing her face in its light and gentle winter warmth. The death of her father would have made her sad, had he been the kind of father one actually mourned. With him gone, Anna now had the opportunity to create her own life in the way she wished. It would be hard work, and she knew that she would need a lot of luck, too—yet she knew, deep within, that life would get better for her.

As the miles passed, and the sun disappeared behind ominous gray clouds once more, Anna's pace slowed, and her optimism faded. Her feet were riddled with blisters, her shoulders and arms ached from carrying her bag—even though she had shifted it from one hand to the other every half a mile or so—and she was bone-tired. She couldn't see so much as a shack anywhere along the road, and it was nearing nightfall. Anna began to fear that she might not find a safe place to stay for the night, so she tried unsuccessfully to pick up her pace once more. The pain in her sore feet was excruciating. "Ow," she moaned aloud. "What possessed me to think this was ever a good idea?"

Turning to look behind her, hopeful that she might see a carriage, or even a cart heading her way, Anna sighed heavily. There had been no passing traffic on the road all day, in either direction, and she could see no movement on the horizon now. She trudged on as the light grew dimmer, her pride and will sapped from the long day's walk and the prospect of a night alone by the roadside with nothing to keep her warm or fill her belly. She stopped by the side of the road and perched on a milestone that told her she only had another three miles until she reached Winchester. She could be there in two hours, maybe even less than that if she could forget how much her feet hurt and walk faster. It would be after dark, but at least she would be surrounded by houses and inns. Someone would surely be kind enough to take her in if she offered her services, cooking and cleaning, in return for a bed?

Wearily, she stood up, stretched, fidgeted her feet a little in her boots, grimacing at the discomfort, and then set off once more. Her progress was slow, and she winced with every step, but she kept pushing on. "I'll be there in no time," she repeated to herself over and over again—wishing with her every breath that it were true. She couldn't have traveled more than another half a mile when there was, finally, the sound of hooves and wheels coming along the road behind her.

Anna stopped and turned around. A large black shape was hurtling along the road, rocking and swaying as it fairly flew over the potholes and ruts in the road. The driver on the box was clad all in black, and he was whipping up his team of two with loud cries and rapid cracks of his whip. He didn't look to have seen her, so Anna stepped into the road a little and waved her hands wildly, praying he would stop and take her into Winchester. But as the carriage approached, Anna could see that he had no intention of stopping. The driver did not quit urging his horses onwards, and the phaeton approached her at a reckless speed.

Anna tried to step back out of the way, but her left heel caught in her skirts. Normally, she would have been more than capable of coping with such a mishap, but she was so weary that her balance seemed to have deserted her and she fell, tumbling into a ditch by the side of the road. She fell heavily onto the knee of the leg that was caught up in her skirt, and she heard a sickening crack as her body finally came to rest. She clutched at her leg and moaned. The pain was excruciating, and she tried to get up. She sobbed, though no tears fell onto her cheeks. It was as if her body was too tired even to do that.

Nobody would ever find her here; she hadn't seen the ditch from the road herself, so she couldn't expect anyone else passing to see it—to see her. If she could at least get back onto the road, somebody might pass by. All she had left was hope, and there was precious little of that available to her—but she must do all she could to at least try to be seen, to be rescued. She pushed herself up on her weary arms and tried to grab hold of some of the wet grass on the bank to pull herself to her feet, but before she'd even tried to put weight on her bad leg, she collapsed back to the ground with a piercing scream.

"How am I ever to get out of here?" she moaned as she cradled her leg once again, and the tears finally began to fall. "I could die here. I must not be so weak. If I have to drag myself out of this dratted ditch, then that is what I must do." Taking a deep breath, she began to claw her way up the bank. The aches in her arms, her shoulders, and her back had been bothering her all day, but they had been nothing to the ferocious burning in her muscles now. Anna gritted her teeth, growling and screaming as she needed to, in order to get herself back onto the road. She was breathless and spent when she finally made it. Her head dropped to the floor, her chest heaving with the exertion, her body paralyzed by the pain that seemed to have taken over every part of her. She had done what she could. It would be up to God and the Fates to decide if it were enough.

CHAPTER TWO

"She threw a glass of wine in my face and told me, quite rightly, that she never wished to see me again," Edward, Lord Westerham said with a grin, leaning back against the plushly upholstered seats in his godmother's luxurious landau as they made their way to Winchester for Sunday Mass. His audience reacted as they so often did when he recanted the tales of his misdeeds. His father, opposite, smirked with suppressed amusement; his mother, sat beside her husband, gave him a look of exasperation; and his godmother, sat beside him, gave a resoundingly contagious belly laugh. He laughed with her as she patted his hand fondly. She always loved his stories of his exploits in London.

"Dear Edward, I sometimes wonder if we shall ever see you happily wed," Lady Frances, Countess Tremaine said, tucking an arm through his and winking at him. He knew she did not mind if he ever settled down, as long as he was happy.

Lady Tremaine was what most people would call a character, Edward supposed. Eccentric, clever as anyone he'd ever met, and always quick to think and act, she did not care much for convention and certainly didn't seem to mind that he showed little evidence of settling down—unlike his mother, Lady Frances' oldest and dearest friend.

The two women had grown up together and had been firm friends for as long as they could remember. They had learned to ride together, to embroider and all of the other ladylike arts—though to hear them tell it, Mama had often undertaken such tasks for Lady Tremaine so that she might bury her head in the books from her father's library. Edward had never met two people so very different, from their habits and interests to their physical appearance. It often made him wonder how their friendship had lasted so long.

Mama was tall and thin with a very patrician manner. Societal mores were important to her, and Edward doubted if she had ever set a foot out of line in her forty-nine years. She was a perfect lady, from her elegant posture to her dainty manners. She drew and painted beautiful watercolors, played the pianoforte with adequate skill and feeling, and sang like a lark. She never argued with Edward's father, or anyone else for that matter. She was docile and did as she was expected, was the perfect hostess, and was never late to anything.

In stark contrast, Lady Frances was short and plump. She lived life on her terms. She drank port and smoked cigars—often refusing to leave the dinner table after supper in order to remain with the men and discuss politics and economics rather than retire to the drawing-room along with the other women. She talked knowledgeably about running her estates, the country's affairs, and could drink as heartily as any man. She was argumentative and stubborn—usually because she was so often right. She eschewed the ladylike arts, preferring to focus on what was going on in the world around her. She ran her home the way she pleased, and heaven help any man who tried to tell her otherwise. And, to her mind, punctuality was something that only ever applied to other people. Edward adored her.

Mama pursed her lips. "I do wish you would learn to be a little more circumspect, Edward," she said. "You are getting quite the reputation for being a flirt."

"Oh, Mama, do speak plainly," Edward said with a grin, knowing that she would never say what she truly thought of his behavior. "I am rapidly heading towards being known as a bounder and a cad."

"I did not say that, Edward," Mama said with a frown. "Nor would I ever say such a thing. I hope that no child of mine would ever be even considered to be such a thing. Why can you not see that people even implying them is most detrimental to your good character?"

"Simply because it is not true," Edward assured her. "I cannot be responsible for the ways other people might think of me, nor do I wish to be, Mama. I may possibly have let Lady Allingham think I cared more for her than I did, but I did not entirely deserve to have wine thrown in my face. I was a gentleman at all times. I cannot be held responsible for that silly ninny's thinking I was about to propose marriage simply because I was kind enough to dance with her once and take her to supper at Almack's."

"He's quite right, Harriet," Papa said, looking up briefly from his newspaper. "The boy cannot be expected to know the intentions of every filly that he dances with, nor should he try. Young girls these days, they all seem to think that every man must be after them just because they have a pretty face and a dowry. In my day, well, things were different."

"Of course they were, Harold," Lady Tremaine said,

rolling her eyes. "Matches were made by our parents, as they should be. And nobody ever married for love, or attraction, or tried to wheedle their way out of a match made for them by their father. We accepted our fate and married whether we liked the person or not—and we made the very best of it we could." Her words were dripping with sarcasm. Edward had to try very hard to maintain a straight face. Papa hated to be wrong and hated it even more when it was Lady Tremaine making him feel small, though he often gave her such easy opportunities to do so.

"Now you are just being argumentative, Frances," Papa said. "You know full well what I meant. Decisions just weren't made on such silly nonsense as how a girl felt when she danced with a chap."

"And it led to so many happy marriages," Lady Tremaine said with a dramatic swoon and a heavy sigh. She giggled, unable to maintain her composure. "Too many women, like myself, Harold, ended up wed to idiots because of the old ways. I'm not saying that things have improved any—but I do think that getting to know the man you are to wed and being sure you like him first isn't such a silly idea as you think."

"But things haven't really changed," Edward said thoughtfully. "Even though it appears that there is a choice, there really isn't for many young people today. They are pushed towards matches with people that are deemed suitable. They must have a title and wealth. They must dance well and look pretty. One's parents still have to approve a match or both men and women face being disinherited. It may appear that there is more choice, but I don't think there is."

Papa nodded his agreement. "And that is why every young girl is simply falling at Edward's feet, because he is

Lord Westerham, will one day become Earl of Winterton. He has a fine estate, will inherit an even better one, and has good standing in Society. He dresses well and is handsome —and has a fortune many would be envious of. He will inherit my seat in Parliament and is friends with Prinny. Any young woman in Society is going to be pushed—by her mother and father, no less—to ensnare him."

"I don't disagree," Mama said, now frowning at them all. "But I do think that because of that, Edward needs to be more circumspect in the manner in which he behaves. It does our family name no good to have him labeled as some bounder."

"Mama, I truly do not think that I will be," Edward assured her, reaching across the carriage to take her hand. "I am respectful, and I am polite. I flirt a little, but no more than any man should. I do not ever promise a girl anything I cannot or will not deliver. I cannot be held responsible for the silliness that they attach to those things in the privacy of their bedchambers. I can assure you that I have no intention of bringing the family name into disrepute." He lifted her hand to his lips and kissed her hand tenderly.

She sighed and reached out with her free hand to caress his cheek. "I do wish, sometimes, that you weren't so handsome or charming. It will be your undoing, my darling boy."

"I shall do my best to be sure it will not," Edward said solemnly, then leaned back in his seat once more.

Edward glanced out of the carriage as the conversation lulled. The carriage wasn't going very fast, as the driver was having to be extremely careful where he let the horses go. The weather in recent days had been wet and miserable. The roads were rutted, and the ditches and some of the fields on either side of the road were filled with water from the heavy rainfall overnight. It always surprised him to see what had once been green and verdant become a lake so swiftly. The flooding made the land exceptionally fertile, but it made choosing the right crops for such land more challenging for the men who made their living from it.

They passed a couple of men trudging by the side of the road, pickaxes and shovels in hand. They were clearly trying to unblock the channels that allowed the water to drain from the road into the ditches and then onwards into the streams and rivers. Their faces were streaked with mud, their clothes sodden. Edward couldn't help feeling grateful that he was warm and dry inside the coach rather than out there in the inclement weather having to work so hard.

As they neared Winchester, there were more people on the roads, some clad in their Sunday best, others dressed for work as if it were any other day. All of them seemed to be ignoring what seemed to be a large pile of old clothes that had been left by the wayside. Edward stared at them wondering why anyone would have done such a thing. Something twitched, making the bundle move ever so slightly. Edward blinked and rubbed at his eyes, sure he must have been imagining it. The rain was coming down quite heavily again, the sound of the raindrops a cascade on the roof of the coach. The view through the carriage window was a little blurred. But when he looked back, Edward was certain that the bundle had moved again.

Perhaps it was just a rat, or something of that ilk, rummaging around to see if there was anything it might eat or that it might make use of for its nest, but Edward wasn't so sure. He banged his silver-topped cane on the roof of the carriage to tell the driver to stop. "Edward?" his mother asked, clearly surprised that he should do such a thing when they hadn't yet reached the church.

"I think there might be someone out there, by the side of

the road," Edward said as the carriage came to a halt and he jumped out of the door.

He hurried to where the bundle lay. As he drew closer, it was quite clear that it was a person, though their leg was poking out at a most peculiar angle. He wondered why nobody else had seemed even to see it. Those on foot were just walking by, shielding their faces from the rain. He supposed they were only in a hurry to get out of the cold and wet weather, so had little time to look around them, but it seemed strange to him that they could walk by someone in need.

Kneeling beside the body, the mud soaked through Edward's breeches. It was cold as ice and chilled him to the bone. Edward shuddered. To have met your end in such a way, in the mud, alone, was simply horrific to his mind. Edward rolled the body over and gasped.

The face that looked up at him was that of a young woman, her hair and clothes utterly caked in mud. Her skin, between the brown streaks, was as pale as milk. She was cold as ice, and her body was stiff and unyielding, as though she were dead, but Edward could see a tiny rise and fall in her chest. "It's a young woman. She's badly hurt—but she's alive," he cried out as his father clambered out of the carriage and made his way towards him.

Yes, it is Anna! What will happen to her? Check out the rest of the story in the Kindle Store! A Family for Christmas

JOIN MY MAILING LIST

Sign up for my newsletter to stay up to date on new releases, contests, giveaways, freebies, and deals!

Free book with signup!

Facebook Giveaways! Books and Amazon gift cards! Join me on Facebook: https://www.facebook.com/rosepearsonauthor

Join my new Facebook group! Rose's Ravenous Readers

Website: www.RosePearsonAuthor.com

Follow me on Goodreads: Author Page

You can also follow me on Bookbub! Click on the picture below – see the Follow button?

196 | JOIN MY MAILING LIST

Printed in Great Britain
by Amazon